"You we_____ you for it, but we're not kids anymore."

"It looks to me like you still need my protection." He lifted his brow to challenge her, hoping she'd take the bait and get fired up. Anything to get her to stop forcing him to confront what he'd kept buried for fourteen years.

"I do," Skylar agreed. "I'm scared to death, but I know if we can get past this and work together again, you'll protect me just like you used to. I've always trusted you, Reece, including that night in October when you held my hand and promised me everything would be okay. You were right. I'm okay. We're okay. Okay?"

"That's a lot of okays," he said, forcing back the emotion welling inside him when she smiled that smile he had lived for back in the day. "I'll do my best to remember we're both okay, the present situation notwithstanding."

"That's all I can ask for," she said, giving his hand one last squeeze. "Now, let's find this guy so I can get my life back."

TRACING HER STOLEN IDENTITY

KATIE METTNER

Harlequin

INTRIGUE

For my Duluth friends.

Harlequin®
INTRIGUE™

ISBN-13: 978-1-335-08212-1

Tracing Her Stolen Identity

Harlequin Enterprises ULC
22 Adelaide St. West, 41st Floor
Toronto, Ontario M5H 4E3, Canada
www.Harlequin.com

Printed in U.S.A.

Katie Mettner wears the title of "the only person to lose her leg after falling down the bunny hill" and loves decorating her prosthetic leg to fit the season. She lives in Northern Wisconsin with her own happily-ever-after and spends the day writing romantic stories with her sweet puppy by her side. Katie has an addiction to coffee and dachshunds and a lessening aversion to Pinterest—now that she's quit trying to make the things she pins.

Visit the Author Profile page at Harlequin.com.

CAST OF CHARACTERS

Skylar Sullivan—A talented glass artist in Duluth, Minnesota, who wakes one morning and discovers her identity wiped away. There's only one person she trusts to help her, but he may not be interested, considering the way she treated him after her accident.

Reece Palmer—A Secure Watch digital recovery agent, he was Skylar's best friend until their senior year of high school. He once thought they could be more, but fate had other ideas. Her accident was his fault, so when she asks for his help getting her life back, he jumps at the chance, even if it means losing his heart to her again.

Binate (010)—The stranger who has assumed Skylar's digital identity.

Silas Sullivan—Skylar's estranged brother. He fell off her radar years ago, but Reece wonders how far out of the picture he really is.

Miles Burgett—A fellow Duluth artist who has had it in for Skylar since several galleries snubbed his artwork by taking hers instead.

Camille Castillo—Miles's partner in crime, who has gone missing.

Chapter One

Skylar Sullivan tapped her card against the screen at the pharmacy and waited while the card reader spun. The word *declined* popped up on the screen. She frowned. That was weird. Her seven-dollar prescription was not going to drain her bank account.

"Sorry," she said to the pharmacist, who was patiently waiting for her to pay. She realized they'd close soon, so Skylar hurried to find her cash. "I've been gone for two weeks and haven't used my debit card. The bank must have put a hold on it. I think I have cash."

"No problem, Skylar. I noticed you haven't been around. Were you on vacation?"

"A working one," she answered, digging in the bag under her wheelchair for her wallet. "I decided to get away from it all and drive to Grand Marais to work on my portfolio. The lake always inspires my nature mosaics, so I rented a little cabin on the shore."

"Well, that sounds like an idyllic place to work, if not a bit chilly for April."

"You could say that again." Skylar handed the woman a ten. "I was lucky the cabin had a great fireplace and lots of precut firewood. It was also accessible, which is rare these days."

The pharmacist smiled and handed her the receipt, change and bag. "I imagine that's always a consideration, but I'm glad you found a way to finish your work. You know I'm a huge fan."

"Thanks, Marguerite. I'm keeping my fingers crossed for a gallery showing soon."

"I'll cross mine, too!" Marguerite said, twining her fingers together before she waved goodbye. Skylar pushed the hand rims forward to the door, knowing she still had another stop before heading to her duplex in the middle of Duluth, Minnesota.

She'd lived in Duluth her entire life and had no plans to move—ever. Did it suck moving around the Northland in a wheelchair in the middle of January? Yes, but there was nowhere else she wanted to live. Seeing Lake Superior every time she drove down the street was her little piece of heaven. The city had everything she needed, including medical care and accessible housing. The art scene was also hopping, and she had her stained-glass mosaics placed in small galleries around the Northland. She sold out regularly, but they also brought in special orders that kept her afloat as a struggling artist. Her goal was to host an extensive gallery showing in the Twin Cities, but first, she had to have a portfolio to back her up. That was why she'd taken the time away to finish some of her tile mosaics. She needed diverse pieces to draw a crowd in a city the size of Minneapolis, where there were twice as many artists as in Duluth.

She could have stayed another two weeks in that little cabin by the lake working on nature pieces, but her friend needed it for her family. Truthfully, while she loved her time away to finish her work, she'd reached the level of solitude she could take. There was never any question that she was the outgoing one in her family. Unlike many artists, she needed human interaction to access her creativity. She'd strike up a conversation with anyone at any given time. That may have something to do with her disability and the fact that most people saw her chair but never saw *her*. Over the years, she'd learned that the chair melted away when she engaged them in conversation, and they'd see her for who she really was.

A smile tipped her lips as she transferred onto the truck seat and connected the hoist to her chair, using the remote to lift it into the pickup's bed. She could break the chair down and stow it in the front seat, but that was always a dirty and wet endeavor in the winter. Not only did the truck give her better traction in the snow for driving up and down the hills of Duluth, but the hoist saved her a ton of time, not to mention wear and tear on her chair.

After a quick stop to drop off some things at her friend's studio that she wouldn't need at the apartment, she headed toward the bridge, dusk gathering at the lake's edges to prepare them for bed after another successful day. Her aching back told her she'd be glad to get home and sleep in her own bed after a long time away.

Her laughter filled the truck as she exited and headed up the hill to her duplex. She was thirty-one, not eighty-one, but someone forgot to tell her paralyzed body that. Her accident had been fourteen years ago, and sitting in a wheelchair all day for that many years tended to be rough on the old vertebrae. Skylar noticed the billboard for her credit union, reminding her she needed to check her account as soon as she got home.

Once parked in the driveway, she hoisted her chair to the ground and did the same with her suitcase, using the chair hoist to catch the handle. Sometimes she wished she had a butler to help her move her things around. Then she'd laugh and remind herself to pack light, because a butler was not in the budget.

Happy to be home, she grabbed her bag and headed to the ramp leading to her duplex. Usually she parked in the garage, where she had a ramp to the house as well, but at the moment the garage was full of art supplies. She would have to bug a friend to help her load and unload them at his studio across town.

A mail truck drove by, reminding her to get online and start her mail delivery again, too. There were so many things to do, but her first order of business was the bank.

She unlocked the door and pushed it inward, surprised when she met with resistance. Nothing should be blocking the door. She'd held her packages and mail, and no one was even checking on the place. Her next-door neighbor, Mrs. Valentine, had a key, but she was unlikely to go in unless there had been a problem in her unit. She certainly would have called Skylar if that were the case, since she was Mrs. Valentine's landlord.

Determined, she pushed harder until the door opened far enough for her to roll in. Once she crossed the threshold, what she saw drew a gasp from her lips. The entire living room had been upended, her belongings broken and ripped apart, and her glass art statues shattered on the floor. She realized a table had been moved in front of the front door to block it, making it difficult to get in far enough to close it behind her.

"I have to call the police," she whispered, reaching for the phone as a text came in.

Still in shock, she opened the text, glancing at it for barely a moment before her eye was drawn back to the living room, where her beautiful art pieces lay in shattered dreams across the hardwood floor. She loved this duplex because of its hardwood floors and easy accessibility in her chair, but the destruction before her turned that love into hate.

The strangeness of the text filtered through her shock, and she glanced at it again. It had come from an unknown caller and was nothing more than a link she didn't recognize. Her finger on the delete button, she hesitated. In light of the carnage around her, she clicked the link. The worst thing that would happen was that her phone would get a virus, but in light of the destruction of her home and its timely arrival, she was afraid to delete it before she checked the link. Her next call would be to the police.

When the webpage loaded, a video started. An Anonymous mask filled the screen, with zeroes and ones scrolling in the background. What sent shivers down her spine was the computerized voice when it spoke. "Hello, Skylar.

I'm Binate. It's so nice to meet you. We do hope you enjoy the redecorating we did in your absence. You've been on quite the tear lately with your vandalism, so treating your home with the same love and affection only seemed right. Naughty, naughty what you've done to those poor, unsuspecting art galleries. I bet you're sitting there in your bright white chair, starkly terrified by the trauma around you, not to mention this message I've sent. Good. I hope you suffer the same way you've made others suffer. I bet your finger is on speed dial for 911, but I wouldn't do that if I were you. It will be hard to prove that you own that house or that Skylar Sullivan exists anymore. I want you to feel the kind of pain that you've caused others. I'm coming for you, and the chase starts now, Skylar. Run as fast as you can— Oh, wait, you can't run! That will make this that much more fun." The voice broke out into evil laughter until it cut off sharply, the screen going black.

Skylar let out a breath, the phone heavy in her hand. She had to call the police but couldn't bring herself to punch in the numbers. Not until she verified that what the text said was true. With a flick of her wrist, she locked the front door, rested the phone on her leg and pushed her chair forward, careful of the glass on the floor as she wheeled to the kitchen to check the back door. When she tugged on the knob, it was locked, which meant whoever had trashed the place had locked up after themselves. A shudder went through her at the thought of someone she didn't know in her home, touching her things and destroying her heirlooms.

Anger filled her. What did he mean by vandalism and pain and trauma to art galleries? Glancing around her kitchen, where every plate, bowl and glass she owned was smashed in a pile on the floor, she imagined the hatred someone must have to do so much damage. From what she saw, the only person suffering pain and trauma was herself.

Remembering what Binate said about proving who she was, she left the kitchen and wheeled down the hallway toward her bedroom. A glance to her left told her that the guest bathroom had received the same treatment as the living room. She brought the chair to a halt at the entrance to her bedroom and sucked in a deep breath at the sight before her. The room looked like a tornado had gone through it. Nothing was where it belonged, and the mattress was slashed open, as were the pillows, feathers strewn everywhere.

Fear rocketed through her, but she pushed the chair inside and went to her safe, her mouth falling open when she saw the door hanging half off the hinges. She felt around inside but found nothing. All her paperwork was gone— her Social Security card and everything she'd need to prove her identity. At least she still had her driver's license. She fumbled with the phone and opened her banking app. What she saw dropped her heart to her stomach.

"No, no. This can't be," Skylar whispered, refreshing the page only to get the same result.

Skylar lifted her head and blinked back the tears threatening to fall. She pushed in 911, but a little voice inside told her to stop, think and analyze the situation. It didn't take long for the complete picture to form, and once she understood the gravity of the situation, she opened the phone app and called the only man who could help her.

Chapter Two

A chime rang through Reece Palmer's house, and he looked at his phone as he chewed his Grape-Nuts. They crunched under his teeth like rocks, rattling his brain until he dumped the bowl in the sink. Chalk another nope up to the health gurus on the internet. So much for breakfast for supper. After he swiped the notification open, he almost choked on those Grape-Nuts when he read the Google Alert.

An arrest warrant had been issued for Skylar Sullivan? No, it had to be a different Skylar Sullivan, he thought as he walked to his desk. Reece sat at his computer and shook the mouse, waking the beast he used for his remote work for Secure Watch, a company out of northern Minnesota that offered physical protection of properties and digital protection of company assets. Reece used to be the muscle, but his boss, Mina Jacobs, had lured him to the dark side with cookies and the promise that he'd likely get shot at less frequently if he worked behind a screen.

She'd been right, too. Reece had been working for Secure Watch for the last two years and hadn't been shot at once, unlike his time working security, which often put them in some pretty interesting situations. Cybersecurity had been his first love when he went to college to study criminal justice. Still, it wasn't until Secure Watch came along that he'd found a home as a cybersecurity specialist.

He clicked the link included with the Google Alert and it took him to a page with a list of arrest warrants issued over the last week. Skylar Sullivan, thirty-one, was wanted for vandalism of several art galleries in the area. Reece opened a tab and googled the art galleries, reading the stories about the vandalism, including graffiti and breaking glass doors and windows. This had to be a different Skylar, the same age or not. The Skylar Sullivan he knew was the gentlest soul alive, not to mention she used a wheelchair and was incapable of tagging buildings with graffiti six feet off the ground.

Reece closed the window and sighed with relief. He'd known Skylar his entire life, and even though he hadn't seen her since he graduated from college, he'd kept tabs on her as best he could. She was a talented artist, and he followed her career even if she could never know it. He shook the mouse back and forth a few times before he grabbed his Secure Watch phone and dialed Mina's number.

"Secure Watch, Whiskey," she answered.

"Secure Watch, Riker," he responded, letting her know it was safe to talk freely.

"What's up, Reece?" Mina asked. "Did you finish that job I sent you?"

"Just about," he said, still wondering what he was doing. "You should have the report in a few. While I'm finishing that, would you do me a favor?" Mina used to work for the FBI, so she had channels that even he could never access when it came to finding information.

"I'll try," she said, as though she could hear his indecision about asking.

"A Google Alert came through for a friend of mine. Skylar Sullivan, thirty-one," he explained. "It's an arrest warrant from Duluth PD for vandalism of art galleries."

"Do you know Skylar Sullivan?" Mina asked, and he could hear her pen tapping on the faithful legal pad alongside her, always waiting for her to scratch out notes.

"I do—did," he said, quickly changing to the past tense. "We went to school together. She's an artist, and I set up an alert to keep an eye on her career."

"An artist is accused of vandalizing art galleries? That doesn't make a lot of sense, Reece."

"That's why I called. When I checked the news stories about the vandalism, I found that some of the graffiti on the buildings was six feet off the ground. The Skylar I know has been in a wheelchair since she was seventeen."

Mina was silent momentarily before saying, "I see" in a way only Mina could say it. She always made you feel like she knew all your secrets. She had probably honed that skill in the FBI.

"That's why I'm thinking it can't be her. My Skylar is thirty-one, born and raised in Duluth, and her parents are Mary and Joseph." No joke, her parents were named Mary and Joseph. He still chuckled every time he had to say their names together. "She had one brother, named Silas, but he's probably dead. No one has been able to find him for years, ever since he left home." He replayed the sentence in his head, and he stuttered. "Not *my* Skylar, but the Skylar I'm talking about."

Mina snorted but didn't respond. "Understood. Does the Skylar, who isn't yours, still live in Duluth?"

"Last I heard, but, oddly, they haven't arrested her yet. The last address I had for her was 1776 West Quince Street."

"Duluth Heights area. Got it. Give me ten. Whiskey, out."

Reece hung up and transferred the files and report Mina needed into a zip file, then sent it electronically via their direct server. No sooner had he closed it than his personal phone rang, so he grabbed it, surprised to see a local number, though one unknown to him.

"Reece Palmer."

"Ra—Reece?" A woman's soft but terrified voice filled the line. "Reece Palmer from Duluth Denfield High School?"

"Yes," he said slowly, wondering who would call him and reference that. The thought had barely crossed his mind when the answer came to him. "Skylar?"

Her quiet gasp told him he'd nailed it. "I—I need help."

"Tell me what's going on," he said, waiting for her to explain the reason for her call. He didn't know why she'd be calling him, but hearing her voice again sent him places he didn't want to go at the moment.

"I was out of town working on my portfolio for a few weeks, and when I returned today and stopped for a prescription, my card was declined. When I got home, my duplex had been completely ransacked, and, Reece, they took all my documents like my Social Security card and everything that proves who I am."

"Who are *they*?" Reece jumped up and grabbed his wallet, jamming it in his back pocket. He pulled on his anorak and swung his go-bag out of the closet. It didn't get used much anymore, but the habit of always keeping one packed when he worked for Cal at Secure One was hard to break. He'd known it would come in handy one day, and today was that day. He hadn't expected that one day to involve the woman he'd grown up with and had once thought would be his, though. At the last second, he darted back to the desk to grab his Secure Watch phone and portable laptop.

"I don't know!" she exclaimed with frustration. "My bank accounts are empty or, at least, they don't exist anymore, and I got a text from someone named Binate who said I shouldn't call the police because I've been a bad girl. Reece, I don't know what's happening, but I'm terrified."

Reece froze in place, his heart sinking the more she explained. "Where are you now, Sky?" He accidentally referred to her by the nickname he'd used all her life but didn't take the time to correct himself. "Are you safe?"

"I don't know!" she exclaimed again. "I locked myself in my duplex because I didn't know what else to do. I don't have any money or paperwork proving who I am other than my driver's license."

"Okay, stay put until I get there. What's your address?" he asked as though he didn't already know.

"It's the same place I've always been. You don't have to come. I can meet you somewhere."

"I'd rather you stay put until I get there. I'm only ten minutes away."

"You'll see a truck in the driveway. It's mine. The garage is too full to park in."

"Okay. Don't unlock the door until I ring the bell. If anyone else shows up, hide. I'm on my way."

After a quick goodbye, he hung up the phone, slammed the door behind him and ran for his truck. Something was rotten in Duluth, and the woman he once thought he'd marry was in the middle of it.

As soon as the truck roared to life, he threw it in Reverse, then headed toward the Duluth Heights neighborhood. They'd grown up there, and her address was the same as it had been her entire life, which meant she must have bought the house from her parents when they moved to Florida.

He blew out a breath and used voice to text to call Mina again. When she answered, he didn't let her speak. "Skylar just called me. Her duplex has been vandalized and all her bank accounts have disappeared."

"That's not all that's gone," Mina said, her voice even, but he could sense her underlying nerves. "Her entire life has been wiped away, Reece. She's in trouble."

Those three words had him jamming his foot down harder on the gas pedal as a sense of doom filled him. He'd let Skylar down once; there was no way he would do it again.

Chapter Three

The doorbell rang in eight minutes, which meant Reece had either broken some laws or was closer to their old neighborhood than he'd thought. Skylar rolled to the door and grabbed the handle, taking a steeling breath before opening it. She hadn't seen him since he'd graduated from college and left for a job elsewhere. She had attended the University of Wisconsin Superior across the bridge for a degree in art, but she had promptly dropped out after a year when she discovered making money as an artist had nothing to do with a degree.

While he'd attended college, Reece had lived at home, which was next door to her house. They'd grown up that way, spending most of their waking hours together as kids, but their social time had become less and less as he made new friends in college and his high school relationships became less important to him. When *she* became less important to him, but she'd wanted it that way, hadn't she? Skylar had told him in no uncertain terms they would never be more than friends, even though he had made it clear several times that he wanted to date her. She'd had her reasons back then. Reasons that didn't seem nearly as important to her anymore.

"Skylar!" He pounded on the door, drawing her from her thoughts as she jumped and yanked on the handle.

The man standing on her ramp took her breath away. "Back up," he said, his words clipped. Once she was clear, he closed the door behind him as he assessed the front room. "Holy hell." The two words were said in one breath before he knelt to make eye contact. "Are you okay?"

"Shaken but not hurt," she answered, inhaling his scent. He still wore Stetson cologne on his body and a Stetson hat on his head, but everything else about him, besides the color of his eyes, was bigger, stronger and sexier than she wanted to face right now.

As he gazed at her from under the brim of that black hat, his one blue eye and one gray eye sparked with the same kind of familiarity she was sure was in her own. Their childhood years ran through her mind as she came face-to-face with the boy who was now a man. Reece, the boy she had called Land because he called her

Sky, had always been tall, but even squatting, he could meet her eyes in the chair. His curly blond hair peeked out from under the hat and nearly touched his collar. It was either a sign that he liked it long or hadn't had time to get it cut recently. She remembered how she used to play with his hair, twirling the curls around her fingers, when she was a little girl. She wanted to do it again and then let her fingers travel to his face to touch the shaped, tightly trimmed goatee that cupped his chin. She wouldn't do that, though, because they weren't friends anymore.

"Thank you for coming. I didn't know what else to do until I remembered you were back in town."

"I suppose everyone knew I was back in town after the Red River Slayer case ended."

"That, but also, your mom told my mom, who told me."

"Does anyone else live here?" he asked, and she could tell the idea that more people might be mixed up in this made him nervous.

"No, I live alone, other than while renting the other half to Mrs. Valentine. I don't know what's going on, but I'm the only one involved as far as I know."

"Good. Well, that's not good, but I'm glad

we only have to worry about your safety right now. Let's get your things and get out of here."

"What? No. I can't leave my house like this!" She flung her hand around at the mess behind him, but he was already walking toward the bedrooms, the ones he knew well, considering he'd spent half of his childhood here.

Reece spun on the heel of what she noticed to be a pair of black snakeskin boots. "You can and you will. We don't have time to clean it up right now. Besides, my friends from Secure One will come in, look around and see what they can find."

"Don't you want to know what's happened?"

"Not here," he said with a tight shake of his head as he mouthed *bugs*. "We need to get out of here. Where's your phone?"

Without thinking, she dug it out of the bag under her chair. As he walked back over, she handed it to him. Did he think someone had bugged her house? A glance behind him at the destruction in her living room made her admit it was possible. The computerized voice started again, and she dragged her gaze to his, his brow up as he listened to the message. A shudder ran down her spine at the laughter. Would she hear that in her nightmares for the rest of her life? The idea worried her, but she bit back the whimper and straightened in her chair. When the video ended, Reece grabbed a pen and paper from the table drawer near the couch and turned back to her.

Passcode, he mouthed, and she took the paper, scribbling the numbers down before handing it back to him. If he realized the significance of them, he didn't say. Instead, he tore the paper off the pad and tossed the phone and the paper into the drawer.

"I'll let my guys know where to find it, and they'll take it to my boss."

"Mina Jacobs?" Skylar asked, not surprised when he lifted a brow. That was always his "explain" action when they were kids. "Secure One and Secure Watch have made the national news multiple times, Reece. I don't live in a cave. The Spiderweb site your friends pulled down still terrifies me when I think about it."

Last year, the company he worked for might have saved the world in a roundabout way. They were involved in a situation on the dark web where one bad actor wrote a program that would slowly give him control over every camera in the world and the ability to collect all that data. The idea of that information in one person's hands was terrifying, and she had looked at security cameras in a whole new light ever since.

"Fair. I suppose that's why you called me?"

"No." She glanced down at her lap rather than meet his eyes. The last thing Skylar wanted to see was his reaction to her following statement. "I called you because even though it's been a decade since we've seen each other, I still trust you."

In a blink, he was kneeling in front of her again, his hands on her wheels. "You can trust me, Sky." His gaze darted left and right, maybe out of nervousness about the situation or because he kept using her childhood nickname despite his apparent desire not to. "Tell me what you need and I'll gather it. I don't want you to roll over any glass and get it stuck in your wheels. Remember what happened that one time?"

Her palm burned at the memory, and she held it up—a long, jagged scar puckered the skin even now, nearly a dozen years later. Reece ran his finger across the scar, sending a shiver of familiarity through her. He had always done that to her, and she was disappointed to know he still could. She'd thought she had Reece Palmer out of her head forever, but it turned out to be more of an out-of-sight, out-of-mind thing. "I suppose a trip to the emergency room for stitches would be inconvenient." Her wink told him she was teasing when she dropped her hand to her lap. "That suitcase is packed," she explained, pointing at the rolling suitcase in the hallway. "I just got back from a trip, but I need more meds."

"Tell me where they are and I'll grab them."

"Lower kitchen cabinet to the left of the sink. But you don't know what I need."

Before she finished speaking, he was already walking to the kitchen. When he returned, he had a baggie full of pill bottles. He grabbed the one she'd set on top of the suitcase, stuffed it in and then unzipped the top of her bag to stash them. It wasn't orderly, but it got the job done.

"Stay here while I take the bag to my truck, then I'll return for you."

"What if we're overreacting?" she asked, rolling aside so he could get to the door with her suitcase.

"Do you want to find out?" Slowly, he raised his brow again as he waited for her answer.

Binate's voice stuttered through her mind, and she shook her head as her heart rate picked up.

"I didn't think so. Wait right there."

Reece disappeared out the door, and she let out a breath for the first time since he'd walked through it. She'd done many hard things in life, but spending the next few days with grown-up Reece Palmer would be the hardest thing she'd ever done.

Chapter Four

Reece slowed the truck and turned left into an area where the houses were separated by acres of land. Each property butted up to Paul Bunyan State Forest on one side and Leech Lake on the other. It was an area of anonymity if he'd ever seen one.

It had been a two-hour drive he'd done in near silence. A glance to his left told him Sky was still asleep. He'd pretended not to notice when she pulled straps from her bag and placed them around her thighs and calves. Without looking at him, she explained it kept her legs from falling open, which was uncomfortable on her hips, and then she'd promptly leaned against the window and gone to sleep. At least she pretended to, but she'd been awake for the first half hour. He knew, because he'd often notice her eyes pop open to see what he was doing.

It was probably the same thing she was doing: trying to forget all the time they'd spent together as kids but unable to stop the memories—both the good and bad. They had been thick as thieves growing up. Not only did they live next door to each other, but all four of their parents were coworkers at a large manufacturing firm in town. They ran, biked and played together. He was an only child, and Sky was the younger of two, but her brother, Silas, was already six by the time she was born, so they didn't have a lot in common.

Skylar was younger than Reece by three months and three days, but you'd never know it by how she bossed him around when they were kids. Her bossiness had always embarrassed her mom, but Reece loved it. He always said she wasn't bossy. She just knew what she wanted and how she would get it. There was something to be said about a girl with gumption, as far as he was concerned, and it had paid off for her. She had built an art empire, even if she didn't see it, and knowing Skylar the way he did, she didn't see it. She had always been driven to be better than she was the day before, which had kept her motivated to perfect her art.

Reece always thought it was strange that he'd had such a close relationship with Skylar as a kid. Their interests were so vastly different, but it never seemed to matter. Sky loved art—any art, from nature paintings to clay pottery. He loved playing cops and robbers, always fascinated by anything true crime-related. He loved comic books that told crime stories, and Sky, being who she was, loved to draw a choose-your-own-ending for the books just in case he didn't like how the original one ended. A smile lifted his lips at the memory. Everyone had always said they were as close as brother and sister, but Reece never agreed. His feelings for Sky had never been brotherly. They'd been something else. Something deeper that he couldn't explain. And then the accident happened, and everything changed.

Skylar had always been a sweet, beautiful, talented young girl, but now, she was a knockout. When he laid eyes on her holding that door open, her ice-blue eyes terrified, he'd lost the ability to breathe for a split second. At twenty-one, she had been thin and sickly, still recovering from the accident at seventeen, but the last decade had changed all of that. She had curves now, and he wanted to run his hands down them to feel her again. To connect with her again in a way that would settle his soul for the first time in a decade.

She wore her blond hair in a ponytail, swinging side to side as she moved the chair around. She had always worn her hair up, and the few times he'd seen her with it down as a teenager always did something to his lower half that gave him internal embarrassment. He shouldn't feel that way about the girl he'd grown up with, right? He'd asked himself that question almost daily in high school, but the answer had never been that simple.

A mailbox came into view, and Reece slowed the truck as he counted off the numbers until he found 1993 Cherry Hill Lane. 1993. That jogged his memory to earlier when she'd written down her phone passcode.

1 1 1993.

He'd been a New Year's baby as 1993 dawned, making his birthday January 1. He hadn't registered it then, but now the number hit him right in the gut. Did she purposely use his birthday as her passcode?

She shifted as though she knew he was thinking about her and blinked her eyes several times. "Where are we?"

"At a safe house owned by Secure Watch."

Her arms went up in the air as she stretched, and he forced his gaze away from how her chest jutted into his space. "How long have I been asleep?"

"About two hours," he answered, turning down the driveway and hitting a button on his truck console. "Secure Watch, Riker." They used the same greeting each time they made contact with each other. If they ever got a communication from a team member who didn't use the code greeting, they knew that the team member was under duress and to send help.

"Secure Watch, Whiskey."

"Mina, we're at the house."

"Garage in three, two, one," she said as the garage door opened. Reece couldn't hold in his laughter as he shook his head.

"Thanks, Mina. I'll be in touch as soon as we're settled." He hit the button again on the console to hang up and pulled into the darkened garage, his headlights illuminating the space around them.

"That's high-tech," Skylar said, glancing at him. "Is she going to shut it, too?"

He held up his finger until the overhead door slid back down behind the truck. "Yes," he answered with a wink. "The house has digital passcodes to lock and unlock the doors and open the garage. Mina has unlocked everything," he explained as he shut off the truck. "Once we're inside, she'll turn the passcode and security protocols over to me. If anyone breaches the security system or cameras, then Secure One takes control of the house to keep the occupants safe until they can get out."

"As I said, high-tech." She lifted a brow at him, and he shrugged.

"Secure One and Secure Watch are in the security business. It's what we do, and considering Secure One's track record with picking up cases that end up putting team members in danger, Cal stopped taking chances with his people. He now has places all over the area to stash people who need safekeeping."

"*Safekeeping.* That's a nice way of saying hiding out, I suppose." She worked at one of the Velcro straps holding her thighs together.

"Life is always about how you look at things, Sky." He winked. "Wait here while I grab your chair."

"Where am I going to go?" she asked, her head tipped sideways until he did a facepalm that brought laughter to her lips.

"Sorry, habit. I'll be right back."

Reece slid out of the truck and stretched his long legs for the first time in hours. The ride had been uneventful, and he hoped his time here at the safe house would be equally so. At least until Mina could tell them who this Binate person was. He'd do his own digging while they waited, and with any luck, he'd have Skylar back home and out of his life by tomorrow. Would that be his luck, though? He'd lived the last decade holding on to the occasional glimpses he'd get of her from a newspaper article or a clipping his mom would send him about her artwork. He'd always assumed that one day when his Google Alert went off about Skylar Sullivan, it would be because she had made it big. Not because she was wanted for vandalism. The thought struck him, and he grabbed his phone. After he opened the alert again, he checked the date of the warrant. It had been issued forty-eight hours ago. She was out of town then, so the police would have waited for her to return to the city. He tucked his phone back in his pocket and grabbed the wheelchair. As of forty-eight hours ago, Skylar Sullivan had still existed. That was an essential part of the timeline.

He lowered her wheelchair to the ground and pushed it to her side of the truck. His truck was twice the size and height as hers, so he'd had to lift her from her chair into the seat when they left. The sensation of having her in his arms again almost short-circuited his brain. She was soft, warm and smelled of lemons and tangerines. Whatever the scent was, it was a far cry from the overpowering perfume she wore in high school. This new scent fit her aura. She was always about nature and the soothing vibes it offered. He'd noticed the soft, breezy linens in her home also reflected that. It was like Skylar Sullivan had come into her own while he'd been away, and it excited him to think he'd get the chance to know her again.

The door cracked open, and she peeked out. "Are you going to stand there all day?"

His daydream broken, he jumped and stepped forward, nearly tripping over the chair but righting himself at the last moment. "Sorry," he said, clearing his throat as though it would be as easy to clear his mind of thoughts of her. "I was checking something on my phone. I'll tell you about it once we're inside."

He moved in to scoop her up and noticed she'd unstrapped her legs while he was getting her chair. Guilt lanced him. It had been fourteen years, but he remembered every second of that night in slow motion. He relived those seconds in his dreams at least two or three times a week. If he was overtired or saw something that reminded him of her, he braced himself for the dreams to come. *The Friday night lights. The crowd loud and rowdy. The breeze on his face as he grabbed her waist, ready to lift her into the air.* He gave his head a shake and cleared his mind of those memories. She'd admitted she trusted him, and he wouldn't let her down this time.

He lifted her off the seat with a smile and cradled her against his chest. He'd been right. Her curves were soft, and when she'd thrown her arms around his neck, his chest tightened, reminding him that Skylar Sullivan still had a hold over him.

Wishing he didn't have to, but knowing he did, he lowered her into the custom manual wheelchair. It looked new and fit her like a glove. The seat reclined slightly, which he knew would make it easier for her to remain upright in the chair, since not all her abdominal muscles worked after the accident. Her legs were supported at the calves by a strap, and her footplate was tilted just enough to account for the tilt in the seat back. The custom backrest wrapped around her ribs to offer her support there, and the wheels were thin, black and, if he had to guess, fast. Sky always loved to go fast, whether on a bike or his go-cart. The frame and back of the seat were painted bright white, and he'd noticed on the way out to his truck earlier that the front rollerblade wheels lit up in rainbow colors with every turn. What he loved the most was the floral overlay on the frame. He ran his hand over the decoration, surprised when it was raised under his fingers.

"I painted it," she answered as though she knew his question. "That's why I went with a white frame. I needed a blank canvas to do my work. Otherwise, white would be a bad choice living in a city where it's impossible to keep it clean half the year," she added with a wink.

"Stunning work," he said, standing and slamming the truck door. "I thought it was a decal, but I should have known better."

Her laughter lit up the garage as though night had turned to day. "You really should have," she answered as she wheeled up the ramp.

Reece pushed the door open for her from behind the chair, and she wheeled into their home away from home. As he brought in their bags and shut the back door, he realized how true that statement was about too many things concerning Skylar Sullivan. He should have known better.

Chapter Five

Skylar studied the man who had dropped everything to run to her aid. It made her insides gel to accept that he was even more handsome now than in high school. It upended her a bit, since she never dreamed that was possible. She'd been wrong. He'd put years on, but those years had been kind. Age had changed him from the beautiful boy he'd once been into a ridiculously handsome man. Then there was the heterochromia iridum—a fancy way of saying two different-colored eyes. Fewer than one percent of humans had two different-colored eyes, and he'd always said that when he got old enough, he would buy a contact lens so that his eyes would finally match.

She couldn't help but smile at the memory of how mad she had gotten about that statement. After his suggestion, she'd given him the silent treatment for two days until he finally agreed never to wear a colored contact. From what she could tell, he hadn't broken his promise to her.

Speaking of the silent treatment, that's what he'd been giving her since they'd settled into the house. *Aloof* was a word that came to mind. He'd given her a necessary tour of the house, showing her the modifications that would help her and what to do if something happened to him. There was a basement, but that wasn't where she was to hide. There was a room behind a panel in the main bedroom closet. It wasn't large, but it was big enough for two people, including her chair. It also held the necessary computer equipment to access help if the situation arose. However, Reece had made it very clear that once she was in it, she wasn't getting out until someone opened it from the central control room when it was deemed safe. She supposed he'd told her that knowing about her claustrophobia, but in a life-or-death situation, she'd take being trapped in a small room over dying. Besides, it wasn't likely to come to that. Sure, whoever this Binate person was had tossed her place, but no attempts had been made on her life, and let's face it, she was easy enough to find. It wasn't like she could outrun anyone for very long. This house, and finding out there were several more around the state, not to mention the underground bunkers, had made it sink in how much danger she might be in. Secure One had battled sex traffickers, serial killers, mob bosses and everything in between. The fact that they had taken her on as a client without needing to be convinced told her she was in hot water. Sure, Reece had been her childhood friend, but if his team had thought for half a second that things weren't as bad as they were, they never would have given him the go-ahead to bring her here.

Reece acted like this was nothing but a job, but she knew the truth. He'd been acting like this since the night of the accident. One moment, he was warm, loving and laughing, and the next, he dropped a curtain of distance and pain between them. It might have had something to do with her pushing him away and telling him they could never be more than friends.

Staring at him now as he sat at the bank of computers pretending she didn't exist, she could still read him like a book. Spinning away from the sight of the man she'd always thought would be hers, she quickly searched the fridge. She was surprised it was stocked with eggs, Spam, cheese and fruit. Was she hungry? Not even a little bit, but Reece probably was, and cooking gave her something to do while he kept his head buried in the computer as though it had all the answers. It didn't, but she'd let him come to that conclusion all on his own.

She had an omelet going in no time despite the challenge of working from a chair in a kitchen that was made for someone much taller. She was used to it now, but in the beginning, cooking had terrified her. With the help of an encouraging occupational therapist who had the patience of a saint, she'd started to learn and believe that she could do anything. That included her art. She'd spent the first year after rehab doing nothing but drawing, believing that it would be too hard to be an artist in a wheelchair. Was it easy? No. But every time she finished a piece, it reminded her that it was worth the extra work and planning it took to complete. Stained glass and mosaics weren't lightweight or easy to move around. She was forever grateful to an "old and grizzled"—his words, not hers—artist in downtown Superior who let her work at his studio and helped her move her equipment around.

With a flip of the spatula, she turned the omelet and added some water to the pan before plopping a lid on the top to fluff it while she cut some apples and searched out plates. Of course, they were on the top shelf, because why not? That was normal for someone who could stand up and reach them. Her—not so much. Skylar flicked the burner off and moved the pan aside before she did what she never wanted to do: ask for help.

"Hey, Reece?" she called out, and he turned from where he sat at the bank of computers and other high-tech equipment that she was clueless about. "Could you help me grab a plate?"

He pushed himself out of the chair and strolled into the kitchen. "You can cook?" he asked with enough snark for her to know he was fully entrenched in his standoffish attitude, but she refused to take the bait.

"Surprisingly, I can do a lot of things." She made sure to make the sentence sound matter-of-fact and not sarcastic. He wouldn't make her feel small to avoid his feelings about the accident. "I wasn't sure when you last ate but figured you might be hungry."

Reece lowered two plates to the counter. "I could eat. You have the first one, and I'll make another for myself."

"I'm not hungry," she said, sliding the omelet onto his plate and adding the fruit next to it.

With a sigh, he dropped his hand onto his hip. "The first thing you need to learn about our situation is this. When you have a chance to eat, you eat. Our entire situation could change in ten minutes and we're moving again. It could be days before you can get a hot meal, so yes, you'll eat."

He split the eggs in half without asking and cut up more fruit. He dropped bread into the toaster and grabbed some jam from the fridge. Backing her chair up, she watched him work, appreciating how his black cargo pants accentuated his muscular thighs. Reece might work behind a computer all day, but he definitely stayed in shape.

The thought made her glance down at her body with a sigh. "In shape" was something she would never be again. At least not at the level Reece Palmer deserved. A T5 spinal cord injury left her with limited chest and trunk stability, which made working out difficult. The gym was great for keeping her upper body strong, but the years of sitting in a wheelchair had changed her shape in a way she couldn't deny. Seeing Reece again reinforced her decision to push him away all those years ago.

"When we're done eating, we're going to call in to Secure Watch and talk to the team," Reece explained as he put the toast on plates and carried it all to the small table in the corner of the room. "Does this work, or is it better to eat somewhere else?"

"It's fine as long as you don't mind that my elbows will be in the air."

Rather than answer, he spun and carried the plates into the main room, setting them on the coffee table. It was low, but that was less awkward than too high. He sat on the couch and shoveled the food in without another word, so she did the same. At least a few bites of everything to make it look like she was following his orders. They made sense, but after the trauma of the last few hours, her appetite was long gone.

The questions spun nonstop in her mind. Who would do this to her? Why had they picked her? Was it someone she knew? How would she get all her accounts and data back? How could she afford to hire Secure Watch? That was one question she could answer. One look around the room told her she couldn't afford them—not their digital work or their protection. Her fork fell to her plate when she realized that she would have to do this alone and had no idea how.

"My parents!" Her gasp was loud in the room, and Reece glanced up from his plate.

"They're fine," he said, his fork halfway to his lips. "Mina checked, and their digital footprint has not been erased."

"They need to know what's happening, though," Skylar said. "They should be warned in case this Binate guy decides to go after them."

"As soon as we finish talking with Mina, she will patch us through to them."

"I don't even know what to tell them, Reece. They're going to be so worried."

"Secure Watch will give them a rundown on what they should do to protect themselves until we figure out who is behind this. I'll be here when you talk to them and make it clear that you're safe and taken care of while we work through this."

Skylar was about to say she couldn't afford to keep working with them but bit her tongue. She would wait until she could talk to Mina and make it clear she didn't have the funds to pay them for this and never would. Reece would argue, but Mina wouldn't. Someone had to be watching the bottom line.

AFTER THE PLATES were cleared and loaded into the dishwasher, Reece checked the house's perimeter using infrared cameras. Satisfied that everything was quiet, he turned to Skylar, who was sitting in her chair staring at a book. Reading it wasn't an accurate description, as she hadn't flipped a page in ten minutes. She was despondent, and as much as he wanted to comfort her, he had to stay hands-off. Skylar was a dream of his that he couldn't shake even though he knew he could never have her. It had taken him years to understand that, even if he didn't fully accept it yet.

It was his penance, though, and he was glad she'd made him pay it. It was his fault she was in the chair. That was something he could never change. If he could get a redo on that night, he would, but that wasn't how life worked. It didn't let you see your mistakes and then allow you not to make them. You made them, lived the consequences and learned not to do them again. Only he wasn't the one living with the consequences of this particular mistake. Skylar was. That was the hardest part to accept. He should be in that chair, and he would trade places with her in a heartbeat if life worked that way.

"Ready to call Secure Watch?" he asked, leaning forward on his thighs.

The look on her face when she lifted her head gave him the answer. "Not until we talk about this."

"Talk about what?"

"This," she said, motioning between them. "You saying two words at a time to me and the grimace on your face every time you look at the chair."

"I'm worried about you. That's all," he answered, forcing himself not to react negatively to her observations. That would only prove her right.

"You're beating yourself up for an accident that was just that. An accident."

"I shouldn't have let you fall."

"Should have, could have, would have mean nothing in life, Reece."

With his lips held tightly together, he forced himself to hold her gaze, to let her see the shame he carried in his eyes for the things that had happened that night.

The air was electric as the cheer teams lined up on the sidelines. They'd made it to the finals, which meant everything had come down to one last routine. It was their senior year, the last year they could compete, and Skylar dreamed of going to a Big Ten school for cheer. Reece wanted to give her that. He grabbed her hand and ran onto the field, lining up with the rest of the team.

"We're in a position to play it safe," she yelled over the crowd. As the team captain, Skylar called the shots on the field after talking to the coach. "Let's do a double backflip lift into a cupie, transition into a scorpion and finish with a toe touch catch!"

Reece nodded. They had perfected that routine this year. He spread the word down the line so the bases and spotters knew what to do along with the other top girls. They'd been working on a new triple back flip into an extended lift followed by another flip to land it. He was glad she hadn't suggested that one. They hadn't perfected it yet, but Skylar never cared about perfect. She cared about wowing the crowd, so he was glad she was willing to keep it simple tonight. His arm was sore from the last few practices, and the last thing he wanted to do was pull a muscle and accidentally drop her.

The announcer called them out to the cheers of the crowd. They were always a favorite in the Northwood competitions and had supportive fans packing the stands. The music started, and the team moved into their positions, spotters in place as Skylar started her backflip. She hit the mark, and he lifted her into the cupie pose, where she preened for the crowd as they hooted and whistled, chanting her name. He took a step back and planted his foot, a sign that he was ready for her to move into the scorpion, where she'd bring her left foot up to her head and hold it—not an easy move on the ground, much less balanced on his hands. After hitting her mark, he pushed her up into the air, her legs coming out in a V as she touched her toes. His head was up and he was ready to catch her, his arms out with spotters on each side.

Then he sailed to the left, landing in a pile of bodies without the girl of his dreams in his arms. Screaming. Who was screaming?

"Reece!" Skylar's exclamation was sharp, and he snapped back to the present, blinking twice before he could even think about swallowing the saliva pooling in his mouth. She rolled the chair toward him. "Are you back?"

He wasn't sure he could speak, so he nodded and hoped she wouldn't notice that his hands shook where they sat on his lap. When she took one in her hands, he knew that hope had been dashed.

"Does that happen every time you think about the accident?"

"No," he said with a shake of his head. "Sometimes I scream your name until I wake up in a cold sweat." He smiled and winked as if that had been a joke, but it wasn't. The nightmares were less frequent now, which he was grateful for nearly fourteen years later.

"Have you talked to someone about it?" she asked, caressing his hand in a way that made him want to pull her into his arms. She was the one who had suffered an atrocity today and deserved to be comforted. Not him.

"Yeah, that's me after therapy," he answered with a lip tilt.

"Reece," she whispered, her gaze dropping to their joined hands. "You have to stop blaming yourself for the accident. There was no way you could have predicted what happened. Who would expect a golf cart to lose control and plow through the team, toppling everyone like dominoes? There wasn't a time that I ran out on the field when I didn't accept the risks I was about to take. Football players had helmets and pads to protect them. We had tennis shoes and miniskirts. We were never going to win against a golf cart."

"You had me!" His exclamation came along with a finger jab to his chest. "You had me to protect you, and I failed." The last sentence was whispered in shame. "I failed you, Sky. You were my sky, and when you fell, so did my world."

Chapter Six

Unable to sit still, he pushed his chair back and paced. All he wanted to do was figure out who was after Sky so he could get her out of his life again. Being with her was too hard. All he could think about was what could have been. What *they* could have been if she hadn't pushed him away. Fourteen years was a lifetime. It was forever ago and just yesterday. He wanted those fourteen years with her back, but he'd never get them. That was the hardest pill to swallow when the choice hadn't been his.

"I know life has never been the same for us, Land," she whispered, using the nickname she'd given him as a little boy. Reece had called her Sky and she had said, "If I'm your sky, then you're my land." And it had been that way every day after until that October night of their senior year. "But you have to promise me you'll stop blaming yourself for something you had no control over. If you can't do that, then I'm leaving now."

His laughter suggested they weren't in a life-or-death situation. "I don't think you're in a position to demand that, Sky."

"Maybe not, but it's time we clear the air once and for all, Reece."

"I'm not the one who pushed you away!" he exclaimed. "I'm not the one who said I couldn't be part of your life anymore!"

He turned back, and Sky spun her chair, blocking his way. He plopped down on the club chair and ran his hands over his face rather than make eye contact with the woman who had been the one to do those things.

"I know that, Land. That was me."

"Don't call me that," he said between clenched teeth.

"Do you think it hurts any less to hear you call me Sky? Do you think it doesn't destroy every part of me to know you've blamed yourself all this time or that you've dealt with PTSD all these years because of that night?"

"It's not PTSD," he said, shaking his head. "The guys I work with at Secure One, yes. Me. No."

"Denial isn't just a river, Reece. From what I just saw, you absolutely have PTSD about October 15, 2010."

Hard as he tried, he couldn't hide his sharp intake of breath when he heard the date. "Enough, Skylar." He didn't speak the words as much as he grunted them. "It's time to call Secure Watch."

"Oh, I get it now," she said slowly, her head nodding as she crossed her arms over her chest.

"Get what?"

"Get why you won't admit you have PTSD or talk to anyone about the accident. At least, I assume you don't, because you probably don't want the guys at Secure One to know, either. If they knew, they might tell you it wasn't your fault. It makes it harder for you to keep punishing yourself for my decisions whenever someone tells you that."

"That doesn't even make sense."

Her snort was loud in the silent room. "Only if you speak a language other than English. I've spent, what?" She checked the watch on her wrist before glancing back at him. "A hair over six hours with you and already figured out that your big, bad, tough cybersecurity persona is an act. See, you try to temper the fact that you still blame yourself for me being in the chair with aloofness and fake aggravation, but your tells give you away. You can't look me in the eye. You can't touch my wheelchair without grimacing. You crack sarcastic comments know I'm right, Land. You know none of us stood a chance."

This time, he met her gaze and held it. "I don't need to let myself see those last few moments. I see them every time I close my eyes. Yes, logically, I know none of us stood a chance that night. Emotionally, it is another story."

"And that's PTSD by definition, Reece. We can't make that part of it disappear, but I also can't sit here and watch you beat yourself up every second we're together. The only thing I can do is help you see that this wasn't your fault. Not when I knew the risk and agreed to it when I walked onto the field. Every game. Every practice. Every time I asked my body to do something that defied gravity, this was always a possibility," she said, motioning at the chair.

"I know that, too," he agreed, still holding her gaze.

"You were always my protector, Land. I loved you for it, but we're not little kids anymore."

"It looks to me like you still need my protection." He lifted his brow to challenge her, hoping she'd take the bait and get fired up. Anything to get her to stop forcing him to confront what he'd kept buried for fourteen years.

"I absolutely do," she agreed. Reece's shoulders deflated, knowing she wouldn't distance to come off as uncaring when the truth is just the opposite."

"Okay, I care!" he exclaimed, unsure what she wanted him to say or do. When she took his hands in hers again, he was sure that wasn't it. "I don't know what you want me to say, Sky. I care you're sitting in that wheelchair because I didn't catch you. There. Is that what you needed to hear? Can we move on now?"

"No. We can't move on until you repeat after me." His huff did nothing to stop her. "Skylar uses a wheelchair." She paused and waited for him to repeat the words.

A hard eye roll escaped, but he answered. "Skylar uses a wheelchair."

"Because she broke her back during an accident that injured several members of her high school cheer team."

"Because she broke her back during an accident that injured several members of her high school cheer team."

"I couldn't have caught her from the ground with a broken wrist."

"I couldn't have caught her from the ground with a...no, wait," he said, rubbing his left wrist absently.

Rather than let him speak, she took his face in her hands. "Close your eyes. Let yourself see those last few moments of that night. You herself from him. "I'm scared to death, but I know if we can get past this and work together again, you'll protect me just like you used to. I've always trusted you, Reece, including that night in October when you held my hand and promised me everything would be okay even when I couldn't feel my legs. You were right that night. I'm okay. We're okay. Okay?"

"That's a lot of okays," he said, forcing back the emotion welling in his chest when she smiled that smile he had lived for back in the day. "I'll do my best to remember that we're both okay, the present situation notwithstanding."

"That's all I can ask for," she said, giving his hand one last squeeze before she backed up her chair. "Now, let's find this Binate so I can get my life back."

"Before we call Mina, I want to run down the situation with you so we're on the same page when we call in."

"I'm not even reading the same book," she said with a frown. "I have no idea why this has happened."

He held his hands up to calm her. "What I mean is, I want to give you all the facts so that you're not surprised by anything Mina might say."

There was no doubt Mina would bring up

things she didn't want to hear about, and he wanted to give her the chance to ask questions when they weren't on camera. He ran down everything he knew, starting with the vandalism of the art galleries and ending with how, as of two days ago, she'd still existed in the world.

"Wait, you're saying there's an actual warrant out for my arrest and the cops didn't try to arrest me? That doesn't make sense. I'm not hard to find."

"That's what I'm saying. I also agree with you, which is why I think, more than anything, it was a way to drag your name through the mud for a hot second before they shut everything down to keep the cops from coming for you. You can't come for someone who doesn't exist."

Skylar waved her hand in the air. "Doesn't make sense. I do exist! The cops in Duluth know me, Reece. They know where I live."

He continued once he grasped her hand and lowered it to her lap. "I know you exist, and so does the Duluth PD. What I mean is the persona they were trying to sell the cops. The person-of-interest alert came out of Minneapolis. It would get filtered to Duluth and they would follow up. The police would come to your house and ask you to ride with them to the station to chat."

"They wouldn't because they know me," she said, motioning at the chair.

"My point is," he said, frustrated by her inability to hear what he was saying, "if the cops did come to your house, you were gone, which meant all they could do was keep trying until they found you at home or they changed it from a person of interest to suspect. Since it was only forty-eight hours ago, they may not have had a chance."

"Let's say that's the case. Eventually, I have to go home. So the question is, how do I prove who I am and that I didn't commit these crimes?"

Each word got louder until he grabbed her hands and squeezed. "Deep breath," he said, and he sucked one in, waiting for her to follow. Once she did, he nodded and spoke. "Remember, Secure Watch will help you, so don't let that fear paralyze you." He dropped his head. "I'm sorry."

"Don't be. I'd have made a joke about it any other day, but I'm not feeling it today."

"Understandable. What I was trying to say before I put my size twelve in my pie hole was to stay focused on the facts. Focus on the things we know are true about the situation. Those facts are that you didn't vandalize galleries, and you do exist. We also know someone out there has a vendetta against you for an unknown reason, but one that we'll uncover with time and investigation."

As though she deflated, her shoulders slumped forward and her head followed. "I know that, and you know that, but the galleries don't know that, Land. I've spent the last decade trying to get a full gallery showing in a city like Duluth or Minneapolis. This will make it all for naught."

"I don't believe that, Sky. Your reputation precedes you, which means anyone with a modicum of common sense will know you aren't physically capable of causing that damage to the galleries."

"I could have hired someone," she said, crossing her arms over her chest.

"You could have, but let me ask you this. Did you have any beefs with the galleries that have been vandalized?" He grabbed a sheet of paper and read off the names.

"Absolutely not," she said, shaking her head before he even finished reading them. "The Duluth one knows me well and would never believe I did it."

"You've made my point then. All I'm asking is you have faith in me and Secure Watch. We'll ensure your chances at a gallery show are still one hundred percent, okay?"

At her nod, Reece stood and walked to the computer console set up for precisely that purpose. All he had to do was keep his eye on the prize and off the woman he was supposed to be helping. Every minute that passed was another minute that Binate had control of her life, which meant Skylar had control of Reece's. While he dialed Secure Watch, he prayed they had gotten to the bottom of it, but one glance at Skylar told him that prayer would go unanswered.

"REECE," MINA SAID when her face flashed on the screen. "Did you find everything you need?"

"We're all good here," Reece agreed. "We had some dinner and I checked the perimeter. How about the other cameras?"

"Everything is quiet, according to the control room."

"Excellent, then official introductions are overdue. Mina Jacobs, this is Skylar Sullivan."

"Nice to officially meet you," Mina said as Skylar waved. "I'm glad we were able to help you out."

"Nice to meet you, too," Skylar said, nervously rubbing her hands on her thighs. "We've heard so much about you over the years. You're like an FBI legend."

Mina's laughter filled the house, and Skylar

noticed it lifted Reece's lips for the first time all day. She was grateful to Mina for doing what she couldn't do right now. "I don't know about all that, but we're here to help, right, Reece?"

Before Reece could answer, Skylar jumped in. "About that," she said, lifting her chin. "I wasn't thinking earlier when I called Reece. I was scared and didn't know what to do, but I also didn't think about the fact that you guys employ Reece or that I didn't know how I was going to pa—"

"You're not going to pay," Mina said before she could finish.

"But, Mina, this house alone must need thousands to maintain every month. I can't even imagine what it would cost for people like Reece to do what they do."

Mina held up her hand to stop her. "The house is going to be there whether we use it or not, so it might as well be used, right?" She waited as though she expected an answer, so Skylar hesitantly nodded. "Then we use it. Make yourself comfortable and don't worry about the expense. What it costs us will be nothing compared to what it could cost you. Am I clear?"

"Yes, ma'am," Skylar agreed. There was no way she was crossing Mina Jacobs. Reece's smirk told her he knew it.

"Now that we have that settled," Reece said,

still smirking, "do you have anything new? Skylar is worried about her parents."

Mina pointed at the camera and grabbed something next to the computer. "I spoke with them a few minutes ago, and they're awaiting your call. Once you speak to them, they will take a little vacation off the grid until this is squared away."

"You think this person might go after my parents?"

"We have to assume they will," she replied. "Whoever this is, they know you, which means they know the people close to you."

"We'll call them as soon as we hang up," Reece said, reaching out to squeeze her hand. "What did the guys find at the duplex?"

"Nothing of much interest," Mina said, looking at the notebook in her hand. "At least in terms of evidence. Iris is working with her phone right now."

"Iris?" Skylar asked, glancing at Reece.

"She's one of our data recovery agents," Reece explained. "If anyone can figure out who sent that video and from where, it's Iris."

"In the meantime," Mina said. "I want you to list anyone who could be behind this."

"The list is going to be short," Skylar said. "I don't know that many people. Artists tend to live in their own little world."

"That just means fewer people we have to check out," Mina said with a wink. "But seriously, I'm talking about listing anyone you have ever had a cross word with. Did you have an issue with someone at the credit card company? Did you argue over a cup of coffee in the Starbucks a few weeks ago? Did you have a problem with a bank employee? That kind of thing. If you don't know their names, write down the companies or branches. We can run those things down easily but need a place to start." Reece looked like he was about to say something when Mina held up her finger and spoke to someone off-screen. "I have to go," she said, glancing back to the screen. "Get me that list ASAP. Whiskey, out."

Reece gave the screen a salute right before it went black. He spun toward her in the desk chair and lifted a brow. "First, we call your parents. Once that's done, we need to talk about that list."

Skylar nodded but didn't say anything. She already knew who he thought should be at the top of it.

Chapter Seven

Reece stepped out onto the house's porch to give Skylar privacy while she spoke with her parents. At this point, there wasn't much she could tell them that would harm the case, so he didn't feel the need to be a voyeur, especially when he still had to talk to her about Silas. Her brother was always a sore subject in the family, and as much as it was a can of worms Reece did not want to open, there was little choice. All he could do was hope she'd forgive him for it.

A hand on his hip, he gazed out over the yard and sucked in a deep breath of the country air. Spring had arrived, but piles of snow still dotted the yard. Before long, they'd be gone, replaced by flowers and grass to mow. Cal had a company that came in to mow and keep the property looking like it had been lived in, even when it rarely saw occupants. He was grateful for it, because moving Skylar somewhere that wasn't accessible meant him being more hands-on with her, and that was something he didn't think he could do. Not if he wanted to walk away from her again once they'd restored her life.

His would never be restored. He'd always remember the feel of her skin against his. The warmth she offered when he didn't deserve comfort. She could believe there was nothing he could have done to help her that night, and maybe that was the truth of it, but that didn't change how he *felt*.

Pandemonium. Panic. Were they the same thing? As Reece untangled himself from his teammates, he decided they were. Screams penetrated the night air. Lights flashed. The sound of the crowd as it pressed in on them roared back to his ears, but what he didn't hear was his best friend.

"Sky!" he screamed, trying to push himself to his feet only to realize his left arm wasn't working properly. He glanced down at it and noticed it hung at an odd angle. "Sky!"

Why were there so many bodies on the ground? He looked left and then right until he heard a strangled cry. "Land!"

He spun, and behind him, on the fifty-three-yard line, was the girl he was supposed to catch. "Sky!" Reece screamed as he ran toward her, splinting his arm against his belly to stem the pain from each step. "Don't move!" Those were his first words as he slid beside her and grabbed her hand. "You're going to be okay."

"I can't move my legs," she whispered, tears sliding down her cheeks.

After a quick glance at her legs, he shook his head. "They don't look broken, but don't try to move them."

"No, Land, I can't—can't feel them."

Before she could say another word, he turned his head and bellowed for help, catching the attention of an EMT.

"You're going to be okay," he promised the girl he'd been in love with since he was old enough to know what that meant. "You're going to be okay. Just stay still. I love you, Sky. You're going to be okay."

Reece gasped and sucked in another lungful of the night air. He'd told her he loved her? He tried to focus his mind on that part of the night, but he couldn't grab the memory again. He'd lied to her earlier when he said he remembered those moments after the accident every night in his sleep. He never got that far. He always woke up screaming her name at the moment of impact. Did he have diagnosed PTSD after the incident? Yes. Had he told Sky that? No. He made sure no one but him and his therapist knew about that diagnosis. Was it shame that kept him from talking about it? No. It was fear, and his therapist agreed. He said Reece's brain woke him at that exact moment each time to protect him from the fear. No matter how hard they'd tried, they couldn't unlock the memory. And they'd tried for years. Then, he spent a few hours with Sky and her touch drew it out of him.

Even a solid shake of his head couldn't dislodge the rest of the memories flooding him. The surgery on his arm that they'd forced him to have even though he didn't want to leave Sky's side. Waking up to find out she was paralyzed for life and would never walk again. Learning that a golf cart had gone haywire and driven right into them as they did their routine on the field. Lying in a hospital bed, being told how half of the team had broken bones and were at hospitals all over the Northland. Ultimately, none of those injuries were as life-changing as Sky's. The settlement from the event had bankrupted the venue but set Sky up with enough money to provide for her immediate needs after the injury and for years to come.

Since his family was tight with hers, he knew that her parents had invested the money so that she got a monthly salary from the fund, and they'd set up another fund to help take care of the duplex with the rent her neighbor paid.

He was glad they had done that, because that money was in a trust with a lawyer and not in her name. If they couldn't recover her accounts, at least she wasn't out all her trust money, too.

Reece closed his eyes and took stock of himself. Was he ready to put the past behind him and focus on the present now? Did he have a choice? No. If someone had told him when he woke up this morning that he would be taking care of Skylar Sullivan by day's end, he would have told them they'd lost their minds. His watch said she'd probably had enough time to finish the call, so he forced his feet forward and walked back into the ranch home, expecting to see her on the couch where he'd left her. Instead, she was nowhere to be found.

His heart pounding, he ran through the house, calling her name until he came to a halt in the hallway. His shouting had drowned out the sound that had always ripped him in two. Sky sobbing.

Gently, he rapped on the bathroom door. "Sky? Do you need help?"

"No," she said, but it was strangled. Reece could picture her sitting in her chair, head in her hands as the tears leaked between them. He'd seen it so many times after the accident, and his impotence in the situation flooded him every time. This time, he wasn't going to let it paralyze him. He was the only one here for her and had to step up.

"I'm coming in. Tell me if you aren't presentable."

When she said nothing, he pushed the door open. He'd thought he was prepared for the scene, but he wasn't. She was limp, with her upper body draped across the lowered sink as though she'd been trying to wash her face and had run out of strength.

"Oh, Sky," he whispered, walking to her and unbuckling her seat belt. "Everything's going to be okay. I promise. Is it okay if I carry you to the couch?"

Rather than answer, she gazed at him, dazed, until he put her arms around his neck and lifted her from the chair, supporting her back and knees. He'd done it so many times when she was first injured. She'd worn a plastic back brace that bit into his freshly repaired arm every time, but he'd never cared. All he wanted to do was comfort her. He hadn't been given that chance, so he would take this one and make sure she felt safe, if only for a few minutes of this wild, unexpected day.

Once they were settled on the couch, he held her, forcing himself to keep his lips closed and remind himself that this wasn't about him. This hadn't happened to him. Sky was the one whose entire life had been destroyed today, and there was no way for him to make that better for her other than to do his job. Right now, though, his job was to comfort her. She would need it for the conversation that was still to come.

The clock ticked off another fifteen minutes of her resting against his chest with her eyes closed as her breathing evened out. Reece wasn't sure if she'd fallen asleep, not that he could blame her. He hated having to wake her, but their work wasn't done for the day, so he had no choice. Holding her again reminded him of when they were kids and she would get mad or sad. She'd cry herself out, rest for a few minutes and then pop up, ready to go again as though nothing had happened.

When she sat up and swiped her hands under her eyes, Reece bit back a smile to know she hadn't changed. "Sorry about that meltdown. After I hung up with my parents, it hit me how hard my world had fallen apart today."

"Nothing to apologize for," he assured her. "After the day you've had, I don't blame you one bit for feeling like your world has fallen apart. How are Mary and Joe?"

"Scared for me," she said with a shrug. "Roman and Mina put a scare in them."

"They aren't a pair to mince words," he said

with a shrug. "Frankly, I wouldn't want them to. We can't be too safe until we know who this is."

"Mom and Dad agreed. They've locked their accounts so no one can access them, which is about all they can do, and they're going out to an island with a friend for a few days. Dad got a burner like Roman instructed him to do, and we have that number so we can update them as necessary."

"Good. I'm sure your mom was frantic to think she couldn't race up here and protect you."

"You do know my mom," she said with a chuckle. "The only reason they aren't already in the car is because you're with me, she said. She knows you'll figure this out. Mom always called you her bonus son."

"Probably because I lived at your house half my life."

"Might have something to do with that," she agreed with a wink. "I need better support."

Selfishly, Reece didn't want to stop holding her, but he twisted to the side and propped her into the corner of the couch anyway with a pillow behind her back. Sky's core back and abdominal muscles were affected by the paralysis, so if she wasn't in her chair, she had to be adequately supported or she'd end up with a back spasm.

"Better?"

Her nod had him climbing up off the couch. "I'll get your chair and then I'll make some tea so we can talk."

"Oh boy. Tea and talking are not my favorite things. Wine and Netflix would be better."

Reece laughed. He couldn't help it. Sky was always witty and ready with a comeback to make him laugh. He was glad at least that much hadn't changed. "I would love to oblige, but life on the line and all that."

She bit her bottom lip as she nodded. "Fair enough. Okay, how about coffee? You know I can't drink that swill you like so much."

"Coffee it is. We'll probably need the jolt of energy anyway. We've got a lot to talk about."

He didn't miss her exhaled breath and muttered words as he headed to the bathroom to grab her chair. "I was afraid of that."

Chapter Eight

Her head was pounding, and she could thank her crying jag for that. The worst part was they hadn't even gotten into the nitty-gritty regarding the list Mina wanted. She'd been thinking about it since Mina had brought it up, and there was only one guy she could think of who might have it out for her this badly.

Miles Bradshaw.

She'd run afoul of him without ever having met him in the beginning. He was another artist from the area who believed he should be the only artist. Miles didn't subscribe to the idea that there was room in this world for everyone's talents. He'd made sure she knew that at their last run-in a few months ago.

The sounds from the kitchen ceased, and Sky glanced up to see Reece walking toward her with a mug in each hand and a bag of cookies between his teeth. She couldn't help but smile at the look of domestication it gave him. The way he moved, even with a bag of chocolate chip cookies dangling from his lips, was like watching a lion stalk its prey. She remembered how he used to take flak at school for doing cheer instead of football. His response was always the same: He'd say running around the field and chasing a ball was a skill. Holding another human being over your head on one hand was a skill at a level they'd never achieve.

It made her smile every time she heard it. He wasn't wrong. Cheer was a sport, and it was a challenging sport that tested your endurance and skill in competition. Few understood that, but they had never cared what anyone else thought. It was a sport they could do together when everything else was separated by gender. Since the accident, people had asked her if she regretted it. Her answer was always the same: No. Nothing in life is guaranteed. When you take risks, sometimes you get big rewards. Sometimes you're disappointed. That's just life. She wouldn't give up all those memories they'd made together because of one night. Those were the terms she came to early on after her injury. Living in the past wasn't living, so she refused to do it.

Except when it came to Land. He was a part of her past she couldn't let go. The ghost of who they could have been haunted her every day of her life. They'd never gotten closure—about the accident or their relationship. Maybe they could have that now. Would she love to have him in her life? Yes. Would she allow it? Not unless he understood that she would never let them be more than friends. Skylar had accepted the reality of her world, but she would never ask Reece to sign up for it, too. That was why she'd pushed him away all those years ago. *You were always my land, but now I am your sky, so use me to be free.*

"Coffee, as you wish, madam," he said around the bag in his mouth as he set the cups down.

"I see you still don't like to make two trips." Sky winked with a smile, which brought one to his face when he took the cookie bag from his mouth.

"Not if I can help it," he replied, picking up her cup and handing it to her so she didn't have to lean forward to get it. He was always thoughtful that way, even before her accident. His friends teased him about waiting on her, but he would turn to them and say, "If you need lessons on how to treat a woman with respect, I have openings on Tuesdays and Thursdays." That memory brought a smile to her lips that she hid behind the cup's rim. Reece wore his

confidence like a fine suit and never let anyone cut him down.

After they'd shared a few cookies, he grabbed
a notepad and sat across from her. "It's time to
make that list for Mina. Someone on the team
will work on it overnight and update us with
anything they may find in the morning. First,
we have to give them somewhere to start."

Skylar watched him tap his pen on the notebook as though they were having a normal conversation about everyday life instead of making
a list of people who hated her. Reece had always been strong, but he was never the silent
type. She could see that had changed. He had
changed. Some of it was growing up, but some
parts seemed to come from a different place
within him—from pain and anger, two things
he still carried—and she could tell it was a
heavy load.

"I've been thinking about it since Mina
asked. The only serious aggravator in my life
is Miles Bradshaw."

Reece wrote the name down on the pad. "Tell
me about him."

"He's a local artist from Duluth. You're his
competition if you color a picture on a restau-
rant placemat."

"One of those, eh?" he asked with a lip tilt.

"Gotta love people with the ideology that the world isn't big enough for everyone."

"That's Miles to a T," she agreed, resting the coffee cup on her leg. Thankfully, he'd put it in a travel mug so it wouldn't spill.

"What is his exact beef with you?"

"We both do mosaics," she explained. "Miles would rather I didn't."

Reece rolled his eyes, bringing another smile to her lips. "I've seen some of your work. Your pieces are gorgeous, and they're always so colorful."

Her insides warmed for a moment before the meaning of the sentence struck her. "You've seen my work?" If that was true, that meant he had been keeping track of her all these years. When she gave him up, it had been so he would forget about her, not continue to look after her.

"Around the area," he said vaguely. "Shops and places. They always have the artist's name under each piece."

That fear seeped away a little but was quickly replaced with the gnawing regret she always had in the pit of her stomach. He wasn't seeking her out, which was what she wanted, so why did it feel so cutting to know the truth?

"That's probably Miles's biggest beef." She cleared her throat when she heard the sadness in her words. "He doesn't think my work should be in these shops. He feels it's deceptive to the customer, despite each display fully explaining how the piece is created."

"Because your mosaics are made from recycled glass?" he asked, and she nodded once. He must have noticed the surprise on her face. "I read the information near the display."

"Right, well, yes. He doesn't think I should be selling something made from 'junk,'" she said, putting junk in quotations.

"One man's junk is another man's treasure." She motioned at him with one hand as she sipped her coffee. "What does he make his mosaics from?"

"Glass, but his are more—" She waved her hand while searching for the right word. "Commercialized?"

"You tell me," he answered.

"It's a good word. There's nothing wrong with commercialized art, but that's not what people look for in the shops around this area."

"Which means yours sell because they are unique and his sit because they aren't."

"If you want to boil it down to one sentence, then yes, that's accurate. Miles's work is nice but doesn't stand out as unique. It doesn't scream, *hang me on your wall!* In fact, several of the galleries have stopped carrying his work altogether."

"If it doesn't sell, they're not going to give it shelf space," he agreed, tapping his pen on his paper.

"Correct. Especially when some of his art was proven to be manufactured."

"As in purchased and passed off as his own?" His brow went up, and she nodded. "This was confirmed?"

"By yours truly," she said with a grimace.

"Seriously?" When she nodded again, he leaned forward. "Has he confronted you about this?"

"Multiple times," she agreed, recalling the last time Miles had cornered her.

"Your expression just changed. Tell me about it."

"You always could read my expressions," she said, holding the empty mug out for him to take, which he did, setting it aside.

"Better than your own mother, she always used to say. When did you last tangle with this guy?"

Reece's words were stiff, and the question was asked through clenched teeth. He had always been her protector. Right or wrong, he'd stood between her and anyone who wanted to hurt her. He let her fight her own battles, but he made it known he was there to wade in if necessary. He didn't care if it was a teacher, friend or family member—no one who meant her harm was getting past him. This situation felt like a full circle that neither of them was prepared for emotionally. Binate hadn't given them a choice, though, and she had to remember it was Reece's literal job to protect her now, nothing else.

"He was the reason I went up the shore to finish my portfolio," she admitted. "He cornered me at a show around the end of February. He'd just learned another gallery planned to stop hosting his work, and he was angry. I get it. It's hard being a struggling artist, but as I explained to him, the galleries make their own choices. I wasn't even hosted in the gallery that dropped him, but he still blamed me. He said I was cheapening the art form by using junk and cheating the system by not paying for my supplies like everyone else had to. That I used my disability as a card to get special favors."

"I was waiting for that. He sounds like the kind of guy who would throw those words at you."

"And worse," Skylar agreed with an eye roll. "He has no filter and isn't afraid to be loud about it. The organizer caught on that I was not enjoying the conversation and kicked him out."

"*Out* out?" he asked with a lift of his brow.

With a nod and a head tilt, she continued.

"There were two days left in the show, but he wasn't allowed back on the grounds. I haven't seen or heard from him since. Several more galleries dropped him after his tirade at the art show. The original one he was carrying on about?" she asked, and he nodded for her to continue. "They told me they hadn't simply dropped his work. They had to ban him from the premises as well. He was hard selling to customers on the weekends, and they were getting complaints."

"Do you go to the galleries to sell your work on the weekends?" Skylar could read his confusion in how his brow pulled down to his nose and the slight tip of his head.

"No. That's why the pieces are where they are—so the gallery can deal with the customer."

"Understandable why the galleries didn't want anything to do with him then."

"I'm almost positive most galleries and shops have dropped him completely now. Everyone talks in that community, and it would have been hard to miss the confrontation between us. Not that I had anything to do with it. I just took the brunt of it."

"So this guy," he said, practically spitting the words through his teeth, "has lost his income stream and wants someone to blame for it."

"And he picked me," she finished. "The gallery owner who started the whole thing by dropping him felt terrible and asked if he could host my work in a special showing. An evening with the artist where I would explain my process and why I find recycled and damaged glass perfect for the pieces I make and how I use it to express emotion in each piece."

"It sounds like an evening I would enjoy," he said with a smile. "As long as work doesn't keep me away, I'll be there."

There was a slight tap in her chest from a place in her heart that she'd shut down fourteen years ago. That one beat, a reminder that the old Skylar was still in there, made her want to cry. She wanted to cry for the kids they once were and the separate lives they were now forced to live. Skylar shook her head, forcing the tears away. She didn't have time for that right now. She was in a race for her livelihood.

"If we don't clear this up, it might not happen." Her voice was strangled, and she cleared her throat again.

"Secure Watch has you, Sky. I have you. No one will get away with this, and we will get your life back. Miles looks like a good place to start."

"The gallery assured me there would be security the night of the event. There would be no way to keep it from Miles once they start advertising it, but they're worried for my safety and that of their patrons."

"I'm trying to figure out where your trip north came into play."

"To get away," she said with a shrug. "To concentrate on my art. The lake always centers me creatively. If I was going to do a private event, I would need a thick portfolio. The time up north gave me that peace where I didn't have to worry about Miles Bradshaw and his vendetta against me."

That word lifted his brow. "The fact that you used that word tells me how serious the last interaction with him was, Sky."

"It's not a word I'm afraid to use about him. Is Miles going to physically hurt me? Probably not. He's tall and lanky, but the only muscle he uses is his mouth." Reece snorted at that comment, and Skylar smiled as she shifted on the pillow. "I don't have him pegged as having the brains to conduct something like this either. He still uses a flip phone."

His grimace was comical, and she laughed until he spoke. "Trust me when I say that means nothing. Many very savvy tech guys know that flip phones are as low-tech as they come, making them hard to trace."

"I didn't think of that, but he doesn't give me the vibes of being the brains behind an operation like this. Could I see him having enough rage to destroy my house the way it was? Without a second thought. Could I see him trying to set me up by vandalizing art galleries? The fact that whoever did it wasn't smart enough to spray the building at a level I could reach makes that a solid yes. I just can't get behind him knowing how to delete my life."

"Trust me, by the time Secure Watch is done with him, we'll know his IQ to the decimal point."

"I have no doubt," she said with a smirk. Smiling and laughing a little in light of the situation felt good. It released the stress and pressure building in her chest and let her take another breath. "Listen, I need to go to the bathroom and lie down. Can we take a break?"

After tossing the pad on the table, he opened his mouth as though he was going to say something. Before a word came out, he snapped it shut again, stood and held her chair while she transferred into it. "Sure. I'll contact Mina with this information, then turn security control over to Secure One and catch a few hours myself. Oh, I didn't think about it with how quickly we left the house. Do you have your catheter supplies?"

"I, um, don't do that anymore," she stuttered, suddenly wishing she were anywhere but there.

"I couldn't deal with the constant infections, so when I turned twenty-one, they placed a supra-pubic tube catheter. It goes through my abdomen into my bladder, allowing me to empty it throughout the day and use a bag at night in bed. I have that stuff in my suitcase."

His shoulders dropped a hair at the explanation, and she realized he'd been genuinely concerned for a moment. "I'm glad. I was worried I dropped the ball on that one. It's nice there are other options for you now to make life a bit easier."

"It simplifies my life," she agreed, staring at the floor.

"Do you need any help getting into bed?"

"No, I'm good," she answered quickly. There wasn't a chance on this side of the grave that she would let Reece Palmer help her into bed. "Thanks for everything today, Land." She tipped her head up to meet his gaze. No longer was the man before her Reece Palmer, Secure Watch agent. He was Land, the boy who would have died for her on that field if he could have.

His eyes darkened when he leaned down and braced himself on her chair. "I should have stopped this guy before he became a problem. You can bet I'll be the one to make sure he no longer is, Sky."

Throat dry and her heart hammering in her

chest, she forced words from her lips. "Land, we don't know if it's Miles." She used the nickname without hesitation. That's who she was talking to now.

"Maybe he isn't, but when he gets a visit from my friends at Secure One, he'll quickly understand that from now on, he's to cross the street when he sees you coming." He pressed his lips to her forehead in a way that surprised them both. "Get some sleep," he stuttered, pushing himself away from her chair. "Call me if you need anything."

Rather than speak, she nodded, turned her chair and rolled down the hallway to the sound of his heavy sigh, which she felt all the way to her soul.

Chapter Nine

A ding sounded, indicating an email had arrived, and Reece clicked over to his inbox. He'd sent Secure Watch the info on Miles Bradshaw so they could do the initial dive while he worked on other things. He hadn't expected them to return the information so quickly. His team was used to working under pressure and for high-stakes clients, so he shouldn't have been surprised, even as the clock ticked toward 2:00 a.m. He had sent the information and tried to sleep, but his brain wouldn't shut off. It just ran him around in circles over the woman sleeping in the other room.

Someone had been harassing her and she had just accepted it as normal. Nothing frustrated him more than her letting someone get away with that. The old Sky never would have. Then again, the old Sky could physically hold her own in a fight. This new Sky? The one who now depended on people more than she ever wanted to, he was sure, couldn't. It would take very little to harm her physically, something she was likely cognizant of at all times. It was easier to sit and take it until someone intervened than push back against the aggressor.

He clicked on the bolded email and began reading the report from his friend Iris. Mina had hired her a year ago when she met her at a doctor's office. She'd been inquiring whether they had any coding positions open and was dejected when she'd been told no. Mina had struck up a conversation with her, as Mina did, and learned she had a degree in cybersecurity but struggled to keep a position because of her traumatic brain injury. Working at Secure Watch was easier because she could work alone and at night, two things she needed to focus. Over the last year, she'd been an integral team member as they grew after the Spiderweb case landed at their door.

By the time they'd shut down the website someone had created to take control of every video camera in the world, they couldn't keep their name out of the news. Before they could take a breath, the phones were ringing off the hook and desperate people were hoping Secure Watch was the solution to their current nightmare. They'd hired several more techs and finally had a handle on things, but it was all hands on deck when big cases broke.

He scanned the body of the email. There was only one Miles Bradshaw who was an artist in Duluth. It hadn't taken Iris long to narrow things down and forward him the information. Reece spent the next hour clicking the links, reading articles and searching his background report. When he leaned back in his chair, he could do nothing but shake his head. The dude was a bit unhinged. After checking out his artwork, Reece agreed with Skylar that his work was good but highly commercialized and not what the art crowd in Duluth seemed to be looking for. There was no doubt that he was talented, but apparently, he wasn't a good listener or observer. If he had been, he might have changed his techniques and found a way to sell more art.

Clicking back to the other tab, he typed in the name of the person he was most interested in. Reece had planned to bring him up last night, but by the time they'd finished discussing Miles, Sky was done. He couldn't blame her. She'd had the rug pulled out from under her yesterday and a lot of information thrown at her. He'd talk to her about her brother after she rested and could look at things more objectively.

There was little objectivity in the Sullivan family regarding Silas Sullivan, but Reece didn't wear those blinders or rose-colored glasses. Working in law enforcement had taught him one thing: if an adult wanted to disappear, they'd either make it look like an accident or fall off the grid entirely to avoid being found. If their body wasn't discovered within a year, it rarely was. If they were still alive and off the grid, the chances of finding them after a year were equally slim.

Reece firmly believed that Silas had left of his own free will. Where he'd gone was still the burning question on everyone's minds. According to his mother, Sky's parents finally gave up on the private investigators and internet searches. They'd realized that if Silas left on his own without providing forwarding information, then he didn't want to be found. If he was dead, there was nothing they could do until his body was located. The police didn't believe a crime had been committed and wouldn't investigate, so there was little the family could do but wait to see if Silas contacted them. According to his parents, they'd given up looking for him years ago. Reece couldn't blame them. Silas's mental health was always unstable, and that only worsened after Sky's accident. Their parents had gotten him help and wanted him to attend college, but Silas was only dedicated to sleeping and playing video games.

After a few clicks, he was into a background program where he started looking for all Silas Sullivans. Did he expect to find him? No, but he had to start somewhere, and at least he'd have this much done by the time Sky was up and ready to talk about the elephant in the room.

"Reece?"

He snapped his attention away from the computer when he heard Skylar call from the bedroom. "Sky, are you okay?"

A quick look at the computer clock told him it had been four hours since he'd started researching Silas. It was almost 6:00 a.m., which surprised him. He minimized the programs and stood.

"I have a big problem."

Reece was in the room before she had finished speaking. "What's the matter?"

"Look." She pointed at her chair, which was listing to the left.

"Looks like you've sprung a leak, my lady." He pulled a chair over and tipped her chair onto its back before he pulled the wheel off. "The tube is popped."

"How?" she asked, stymied. "It's just been sitting there."

"If I had to guess," he said, lowering himself

to the end of the bed. "A piece of glass from your house yesterday is the culprit."

"Land, I mean, Reece, I used the chair for hours after that."

"You did," he agreed, not commenting on her use of his nickname. He didn't care what she called him as long as she was safe. "But it could have taken that long of you rolling the chair over the spot on the tire before it nicked the tube." The tire was so flat that he could easily pull it off the rim, and, sure enough, a shard of glass fell out.

"There's a tube in my suitcase," she said as he showed her the split-open inner tube. "I always carry spares, but the tire is a problem."

"I don't think so," he said, running his thumb along the inside of the tire until he found a small slit. "It cut the tire slightly, but that's easy enough to fix. There's some epoxy in the garage that I can use. Once I'm done, I'll return to help you get ready while the tire dries, but the chair will be out of commission for an hour."

"Sure, go ahead. I'll wait here," she said with a tight smile.

"I'll be right back," he promised, grabbing the tire and the old inner tube and heading for the door.

"Reece?" He paused by the door and turned back to her. "Thanks."

"I told you, we've got you. There's no need to thank me every time."

"That's where you're wrong," she said, resting her head on the pillow. "But you'd have to be in my shoes to understand why."

All he could do was nod once in understanding and head to the garage to MacGyver his ex–best friend's wheelchair tire so they could make a fast getaway if the need arose. All he could think was *Sometimes, life is weird.*

SETTLED ON THE couch after a breakfast of pancakes and coffee, Skylar watched Reece working in the kitchen as he cleaned up. His casual humming as he wiped down the counters and washed the dishes made it seem like any other morning in any American household, but that would never be them. Especially since they were hiding out in the middle of nowhere while trying to figure out who had imploded her life.

Sky inhaled a deep breath and noted the slight twinge in her chest. She'd cried herself to sleep last night, her face buried in a pillow so the man who had come to her rescue wouldn't hear her. The last thing she wanted was to end up in his arms again. Check that. She wanted to be in his arms, but she understood what a bad idea it would be if she wanted to get through this and go back to her life without him. Her life was already dull and lonely. When she returned to her duplex, it would feel nothing but desolate now. She'd already been considering a move to a bigger city but had vetoed it because accessibility was unaffordable for a starving artist.

Sure, she could use her settlement money to set herself up somewhere, but she wanted that money to last as long as possible, and her life in Duluth would allow for that. Maybe she just needed a change in scenery. When this was over and she could move around the world again as Skylar Sullivan, she'd buy a plane ticket and visit her parents in Florida. A little sunshine on her face would be welcome after all this.

"Can I get you anything?" Reece asked as he walked into the living room.

She glanced up, surprised by his presence. "Do you have a piece of paper? I thought of a design. I want to draw it out so I don't forget."

"There must be something here somewhere," he said, glancing around the computer setup. "Wait, I know. Be right back."

When he disappeared down the hallway, she pushed herself back into the couch and propped the pillows under her knees that had shifted. When she wasn't in her chair at home, she had a lift recliner that she sat in, which kept her trunk and back supported. Here, she had to improvise to keep herself from getting sore.

"I noticed this last night in my bedroom," he explained, handing her a sketch pad. "Charlotte must have left it here."

Skylar took the pad from his hand and flipped it open. It contained several sketches that looked like the start of a logo. "Charlotte was the one who killed the Red River Slayer, right?"

"Yeah, Charlotte Holbock," he said, sitting in the desk chair. "With her husband, Mack, they tracked him down and unexpectedly took him out. She won a presidential citizen medal for her involvement in the case."

"She's a great artist, too," Skylar said, pointing at some of the other drawings. She pulled a pencil from her pocket and opened a new page as he snorted. When she glanced up, he was smiling. "What?"

"You carry a pencil in your pocket."

"I'm an artist. Of course I carry a pencil in my pocket. There are also several in my chair bag and my truck, and sometimes I stick one in my hair just in case."

"Just in case all the rest desert you?"

"More like an emotional support pencil," she said, scratching out the image she'd pictured last night. "What exactly do you do for Secure Watch? Are you like a hacker or something?"

His laughter filled the room, and it lifted her

lips, too. "No, I leave the hacking to Mina, Delilah and Kelsey. I'm what they call a digital forensic examiner. I get to solve mysteries."

"You always loved a good mystery book as a kid," she said with a smile, remembering all the choose-your-own-adventure books they used to read together.

"I love solving puzzles, and this job lets me do it day after day. When a company has a problem, I get the information from their devices and try to learn how the unauthorized person accessed the system. It's my job to follow the trail and gather all the evidence for trials and that kind of thing. It's rewarding work."

"It's the kind of work no one thinks about anyone doing, to be honest. You assume you're safe online when that's anything but the truth. Case in point," she said, dropping her pencil to motion around the room.

"You nailed it. The cases we've been involved with over the years have unintentionally taught people that, I think. It's been hard for Cal. He went from being a small security group installing perimeter cameras to being thrust into the spotlight without being equipped to deal with the influx of business. He stepped up and kept evolving. That's all any of us can do in a world like this. What are you drawing?"

She turned it to face him. "We passed some

sandhill cranes on the way here yesterday. They were standing there watching their baby waddle about. I've never done sandhill cranes before, but they inspired me."

"What are all the letters and arrows for?"

Lowering the pad to her lap, she pointed to the tallest crane. "Those are notations telling me what color glass to use or what technique to use on the glass to shade it."

"The way you do art has always fascinated me," he said, leaning forward and clasping his hands in front of him. "Listen, we need to talk."

She knew it was coming. They'd been awake for an hour and had made small talk but avoided the real reason they were there. They couldn't keep doing that if they were going to solve this problem so she could move on with her life.

"I know it's time, but I'm nervous."

"It would be weird if you weren't nervous," he promised. "That's normal, but remember you have an entire team behind you and they're working round the clock to find out who is behind this. Last night, while you were sleeping, Iris sent me the background information on Miles Bradshaw. Interesting guy, and not in a good way." She held her hand out to him as if to say, *Right?* "They're doing a deeper dive into him now that I highlighted some areas for them to focus on."

"What kind of areas?" she asked, setting the pad on the coffee table. Relaxing time was over. She needed to dig in and help Reece. People she didn't even know were trying to get to the bottom of this, so the least she could do was help.

"To start, his increasingly aggressive interactions with other artists and gallery owners. He also has some history of petty crimes and such. The team will ensure there aren't other accusations about more significant crimes against galleries or people."

"I still find it hard to believe that an artist would damage galleries just to get back at me," she said, her shoulders falling forward. "It's hard enough to keep art galleries open, so destroying them only makes it harder for everyone in the art community."

"I would say that I agree, and I do to a degree, but I've also worked with a lot of narcissistic individuals. Many believe that if they can't be involved in something, no one can. If that makes sense."

"It does," she said with a nod. "Miles certainly fits that bill. The amount of rage exhibited in my home yesterday makes me want to vomit, but it also tells me whoever did it was focused on my art."

"How so?"

Skylar pulled herself back up against the

cushion to get comfortable. He must have noticed, because he moved beside her on the
couch and braced her feet against his thigh so
she wouldn't keep sliding down.

"Thanks," she said with a relieved smile. "It's
hard to sit like this."

"I understand. I'll have your chair ready
soon. The art?"

Her nod told him her head was back in the
game. "What I meant was, the house was
tossed, but if you looked around, my art took
the brunt of it. Every mosaic and glass piece
was shattered. All the paintings or sketches
were ripped apart and shredded."

Reece was quiet for a few moments before
he nodded. "You're right. I was focused on the
whole picture, but it's obvious when you break
it down. That leads me to my next question."

"Which is?"

"Silas."

The name slammed into her like a thousand
bullets that she wasn't sure she'd survive.

Chapter Ten

It was easy to be mad at him for bringing him up, but Skylar knew it was inevitable. You can't have a skeleton that size in your closet and not expect someone to want to take a peek. "We don't need to involve him. He's dead and gone, Reece."

"Gone? Yes. Dead? Maybe not."

"He's been gone for thirteen years, Reece. He's dead. A John Doe in someone's morgue or buried in a potter's field somewhere. Leave it alone."

"We have no evidence that he's dead," Reece argued. "When did your parents stop looking for him?"

Her shrug was jerky as she did the math in her head. "Probably nine or ten years ago? There wasn't much sense in paying someone to look for a kid who didn't want to be found. As parents, that was hard for them to accept, but let's not mince words here. Silas had problems.

We can't and never did deny that was part of the situation." The following sentence would take him by surprise, but she had to tell him. "Silas didn't even graduate from high school."

"What? No, I remember that he did," Reece said, turning to face her better. "Your mom had a party and the whole thing."

"Silas walked the stage and there was a party, but that diploma case was empty. He had two credits he was supposed to finish that summer and then they'd mail him the diploma, but he never went to summer school, so he never got the diploma. That's why he worked low-wage jobs and just drifted around. My parents tried to help him. They found ways for him to get his diploma, but he refused to do any of them. Eventually they gave up, deciding he was an adult and had to make his own decisions."

"Which is why they stopped looking for him, too?"

She made the so-so hand motion. "In a way, yes. When Silas left home, we thought something bad had happened, but there was no evidence of that. The police could locate his car on traffic cameras throughout the state, but when he didn't return in a few months, Mom called the police again. They insisted there was no evidence of a crime or foul play, so they couldn't get involved. Private detectives came up empty-handed every time they hired one. Our family therapist finally sat everyone down and suggested that maybe Silas left because he wanted a fresh start. After my accident, life was difficult for a few years, and as an adult, he didn't have to stay there and live through it, too."

"He could have left a note," Reece said through clenched teeth.

"Silas could have done a lot of things he didn't do, Reece. That was the nature of the beast with him. It was hard for my parents to detach themselves enough to see their son for who he was. That's just being a parent. I never liked him, so that gave me clarity they didn't have. It was hard to hide my relief when he didn't return after a few weeks."

His shoulder tipped in agreement. "You know how I felt about him."

It released some tension in her chest when she laughed, which felt good considering the situation. "You never made it a secret that you'd like to take Silas to an island and leave him there."

That made him smile. "He wasn't my favorite guy, but I still believe we must do our due diligence where he's concerned. I don't need your permission, but I want us to discuss it so you're prepared for what we might find."

A heavy sigh escaped, and she tossed her

head back on the pillow to avoid eye contact with him. "Do what you have to do regarding Silas. I'll continue to believe this has nothing to do with him. Even if he is alive, he doesn't have the base knowledge to pull off a quarter of what this Binate guy has done in the last twenty-four hours, but you do you."

"Thanks, I will," he said with a wink when she sat up again. "Now that we have that settled, we need to do a deep dive into your social media accounts."

"That's going to be difficult since I can't access them."

"You can't, but one Mina Jacobs can. She's working on it right now and will call me when she's in. While we wait, I'll fix your wheel so we're mobile should we need to be."

With a nod, he headed for the garage, and Skylar flopped her head back on the pillow again. There was no way Silas was behind this, right? She'd never had any illusions about who her brother was, even as a kid. He'd shown his true colors to her at an early age. Growing up, she had very few memories of her brother. He was always on the outer edge of their family. She could only describe it as he was there to cause problems and stir up resentment but emotionally checked out. Was it intentional to treat him as an outsider? It was for her. She was positive that if Land hadn't walked in on them one day when she was in the seventh grade, her brother would have crossed a line and done something that would have torn their family apart. Land may have been young, but he was loud. By the time he finished with Silas for touching her, Silas had a black eye, a busted lip, a concussion and a healthy respect for keeping his hands off his sister. Unfortunately, it also filled Silas with rage, which he carried for them for too many years. Skylar's parents had put Silas into therapy immediately and made sure their daughter was never alone with him again, but that only made matters worse for her.

The Sullivan household had always been tense, something she hadn't realized until Silas left home, but it got worse as soon as Silas hit puberty. That was why Skylar had gotten involved in cheer at such a young age. It gave her an escape she needed from the angry young man who often refused to leave his room for days, screamed at their parents and repeatedly got in trouble at school. Skylar always thought it was a case of any attention being good attention, but the weird part was that their parents were good parents. They loved them both equally and didn't play favorites. Silas didn't want love, though. He wanted power and control, at least if you listened to him. He took his hatred out on her for ruining the control he had over their parents for the first six years of his life.

The only reason she understood all this was due to the years of family counseling. Between the accident and Silas leaving, their family was in shambles. At the time, Reece's mom had gently reminded them that their work benefits covered therapists, so maybe it was time to visit one. Skylar had agreed immediately. Her father took a bit longer to convince, but eventually, they'd found a counselor who helped them see that what happened with Silas was no one's fault but his. They'd done their best to help him, but he'd refused all help and chosen to go it alone. Families fall apart all the time, and the only way to move forward is to accept that person's decision as their own and continue to live your life. If you don't and instead focus all your time and energy on someone who doesn't want or deserve it, your life is no longer your own.

It had taken her parents two more years to accept that, but everyone's lives improved once they did. They had retired from their jobs in Duluth and moved to Florida, where they'd invested money into a small marina. Her father had always loved boats and the water, and the new business allowed him to enjoy both at a slower pace. Her mom grieved the little boy she remembered, but she accepted that he was an adult now and that they couldn't change who he was.

The idea of letting Reece dig Silas back up after they'd buried him as a family rankled her. He didn't have the right to tell her she had blinders on when it came to her brother, because she didn't. She was fully aware of who and what her brother was. As in past tense, because whether he still sucked air or not, he was dead to her. He had been for most of her life. But she knew Reece. He wasn't going to let this go until he proved one way or the other whether Silas could somehow be involved in the destruction of her life. The implications of finding Silas alive hit her, and she groaned. She would have to tell Reece the truth about him, because if she knew one thing, it was this: Silas Sullivan had to remain dead, or their entire family was at risk.

REECE TAPPED HIS pen on the desk as he pored over the information about the nationwide network of crimes against art galleries. He'd be mad about it, but it was too laughable to think anyone would believe that Skylar was capable of something like this. She was so physically incapable of almost all the damage that he was starting to suspect that might be why the cops hadn't knocked on her door. It wouldn't take much underlying investigation to see she couldn't do this, and she was right when she said the cops in Duluth knew her. That might have been why they hadn't pulled her in yet.

They'd watched the original Binate video again after Mina sent a copy, but the voice was electronic and the figure behind the camera could have been his own father. Skylar couldn't say it was Miles Bradshaw, but she also couldn't say it wasn't, which was precisely what this person wanted. He wanted them to think everyone was a suspect so they could never narrow in on him. If Reece had to guess, Binate had been expecting Skylar to go to the police when she got that video, not the premier cybersecurity group in the nation. Maybe Binate should have done a little bit more research on who Skylar's friends were before he decided to take her on.

Were they friends, though? For the last fourteen years, he didn't know what they were. They weren't friends, but they also weren't frenemies. Reece couldn't speak for Skylar, but he could say with certainty that he had thought of her every single day since he'd last seen her. It was impossible not to when half of him was missing every second of the day. While he couldn't speak for her, since she was the one who pushed him away, he still considered them friends.

Sky had pointed out that whoever this was, they thought she was far more capable than she was. At first, he'd thought she was trying to explain why she'd pushed him away, but when he put that aside and listened—really listened—that wasn't what she was saying at all. She was saying that there was no way she could travel alone by car for long distances. She certainly couldn't fly and keep a low profile when she had to check her chair and be carried on and off the plane. She could not roll around these buildings, spray painting and breaking glass from a wheelchair without being noticed. Short of hiring someone to do the crimes, it was unrealistic to believe Skylar was involved.

The sick soul that dreamed up this scheme either didn't know about her limitations or was hoping people would think she'd hired someone to do it and just wanted to ruin her reputation. It also made her a persona non grata within the art world. Unless they could prove this wasn't her, she'd never be invited to hold a gallery showing with these accusations hanging over her head. That's what made him lean toward Miles Bradshaw as the instigator. It seemed he'd do anything to sideline her career. The sticking point for him was that Miles knew her and could see her limitations, even if he didn't understand them. Then again, he didn't have to understand them to ruin her reputation. All he had to do was convince people she was behind it. On the other hand, Silas had taken off so early in Skylar's recovery that he might not know her limitations, but he also might not care.

"When is Mina calling?" Skylar asked as she rolled into the room, breaking him from his spiraling thoughts.

When Reece turned to face her, he couldn't help but drink her in. She would always be the girl next door, but she was also stunning in the simplicity of her style. She wore floral boho pants and a blue-green blouse that drew his eye to hers. Her eyes told him she was still terrified, but he also saw determination. When she gazed at him, he wanted to believe he saw desire in her eyes, but he couldn't let himself go there. She'd made it clear they could never be more than acquaintances, and once she was clear of Binate, he would have to let her go again.

Self-preservation had him turning away before he answered. "Mina will be calling any minute." An electronic tone rang out. "Speak of the devil. Are you ready? This won't be easy, but with any luck, she has the information we need to get your life back."

He waited, watching the fear, anger and determination roll across her face before she nodded. "I'm ready. It's time to end this so we can return to our lives."

As Reece pressed the button to respond to Mina, all he could think was that was the last thing he wanted to do.

Chapter Eleven

"We have a problem," Mina said as soon as Reece connected with her.

"Thanks, Captain Obvious," he said with a wink. Sky had wheeled beside him in front of the computer monitors, ready to sort through her social media posts.

Mina offered a rare grin that said she was amused. "My apologies. We have a new problem."

"Fantastic, because why not?" Sky asked, rolling her eyes.

"Enlighten us," Reece said, grabbing a pen and pad of paper. "How big of a problem is it?"

"He knows where you are."

"Impossible," Reece said, his heart rate ticking up at the thought. "It's been calm and quiet here all night."

Mina held up her finger and grabbed her tablet, tapping around on it while she kept one eye on the camera. "I was able to tap into her Facebook account. He's using it as a vlog of sorts."

"Whatever for, if no one can access it?" Sky asked, her head tipped in confusion.

"We'll get to that. But—" Mina flipped the tablet so they could see the screen. Binate was in front of the camera. Reece felt a shudder go through Sky, and he put his arm around her back to ground her. If Mina noticed, she didn't react. Instead, she pushed the play button, and Binate's electronic voice filled their space again.

"It's cute how you think I don't know where you went with that agent, Skylar. I know everything about you, including your address—1993 Cherry Hill Lane is so far out in the sticks that calling for help would be futile. I'd have you before the cops could even circle their wagons. Oh, sure, you think you're safe hiding there with an ex-cop, but I'm not afraid to hurt him to get to you. Bide your time, Skylar, I'm coming for you. It's too bad you'll never see this and know that. Then again, I do love a good surprise." The video ended with an electronic horror laugh that sent a shudder down his spine.

"My truck is clean," he said the moment Mina put the tablet down. "I have a device that tells me if any GPS was tacked to the truck."

"You might be clean, but I'm not entirely sure that Skylar is," Mina said, glancing at her.

"You left your phone, but did you take anything else?"

"Just the things that were in my suitcase from my trip north and my chair."

Reece raised a brow at the camera, and Mina nodded. "I'll wand the chair." He jumped up and jogged to the garage, cursing himself the whole way. Why the hell hadn't he checked her chair before they left Duluth? They all carried wands to check for bugs and GPS clips. He knew the answer—he'd dropped his guard when he'd come face-to-face with Sky again. Big mistake. Big, big mistake. Mina would have words with him about this if they found a tracker. When he ran back in, he was already addressing the camera. "Rookie move, boss, I know. Dammit, I should have checked before we left."

"Relax, Reece. It was a situation that required you to get her out of there quickly, which doesn't always leave us time to think clearly. I also didn't think to remind you, so I'll share the blame if you find one."

Reece offered her a smile of appreciation. She was right, but that didn't make him feel any better about forgetting something so important.

"I think I'd know if it was in my chair. I'm never without it, and there aren't a lot of places to hide something where I wouldn't find it. How long do they even stay active?"

"Depends on the kind," Mina said. "Some are solar powered and can last up to thirty days."

After taking in the wheelchair, he knew. "The bag," he said, running the wand over it. Sure enough, the wand beeped.

Sky looked up. "The bag is always there. I have to carry things."

Reece ran it over the bag again several times, the beeping louder each time until he was right over it. He wanded the rest of the chair for completion's sake but got no other hits.

"Aren't you going to get rid of it or something?" Sky asked when he put the wand down.

"No." He shook his head as he took her hand. "It will stay where it is until we decide what happens next. Then, when we're ready to go, we'll put the entire bag beside the bed. If I lift the tracker out, he'll know we found it. We need to get out of here before he catches on."

Mina nodded, agreeing. "Leave everything in place and the lights on. Sky, can you duck low enough in the truck to not be seen?"

"I'd have to be on my side with my legs propped, but if he covered me with a blanket and it was dark, you wouldn't see me."

"Do that until you're clear of the place,"

Mina told Reece. "Can you hide the chair in the truck?"

He glanced at Sky for confirmation.

"If we take the wheels off and fold the back down, it would be lower than the back of the truck. A tarp would then hide it."

"To what end, boss?" Reece asked in confusion.

"If the perp is watching the house, he may approach if he sees you leave alone, with all the lights still on. It's worth a shot to see if he bites. If he gets into the house, I can trap him there until the police arrive."

"It's worth a shot," Reece said with a nod. "We need another place to go. Should I take the portable equipment so I can contact you?"

"Normally, yes, but it's time for you to come home. We have an empty cabin since Delilah and Lucas moved to Wisconsin. It's not perfectly accessible, but it will be better than a hotel room, and you'll have access to the equipment in the command center."

"I don't want to bring trouble to Secure Watch," Sky said, glancing between him and Mina. "I can't put all of you in danger, either."

His laughter filled the room, and he gently shoulder bumped her. "Sweetheart, that's the very last thing you need to worry about. Let

Binate show up on Secure Watch's doorstep. It will be the last thing he does as a free man."

Mina shot him a finger gun and a wink. "Normally, I'd tell you to watch your tail, but in this case, I won't. If you bring along an unwanted pest, we'll swat him and take care of the problem by daybreak. Do be careful, though—the guy is unpredictable. Stay aware."

"You got it, boss. It will take us a few to get ready."

"Once you're in the truck, call in and I'll take control of the house. See you in two hours. You can get some sleep and then go over the dupe I made of her Facebook page."

"You said we'd get to why he would put up videos that no one could watch," Sky said, glancing between Reece and Mina.

"You can look at that page as well." Mina nodded. "He's started a page on Facebook calling for your arrest for all the gallery crimes."

Reece paused what he was doing to tip his head at his boss. "The page is set up like a petition?"

"It's more like a hate page," Mina explained. "He's posting pictures of the galleries after the crimes."

"Listen," Sky said with a shake of her head. "I'm not a big name in the art world. Literally no one outside of Duluth even knows who I am."

"While that may be true, he's working hard to change that," Mina explained. "He's hanging out all the dirty laundry he can find about you. Whether any of it is true or not isn't what matters. What matters is convincing the public that it is."

"Is he having any luck with that?" Reece asked, anger filling his veins until his blood boiled and his ears turned hot.

"Not that I can see. As I said, we'll look at it when you get here. I can't convince Facebook to shut it down because he set it up as a business page using your personal page to do it, so to them, it looks legit."

"But it's my page!" Sky exclaimed, and Reece could tell she was holding back tears of anger and anguish.

"It is, but he changed the name and deleted all of your postings, so it doesn't look like it was ever your page."

"I don't understand how he could do that," Sky said, her tone telling Reece she was hitting the end of her ability to reason. Since he still had to get her to safety, he glanced at Mina, who nodded in agreement.

"I'll explain that on the way," Reece said. "We need to get out before we can't."

"I thought you said everything is quiet," Sky said, the words filled with nerves.

"It is," Mina said patiently. "And we want to keep it that way, so it's time to move. Will you be ready in ten?"

With a nod, Mina disconnected. Reece took Sky's hand to calm her. "I got you. Secure Watch is behind us, so don't be afraid."

"Too late," she whispered, her smile watery. "That ship sailed."

"I've let you down once, Sky. It won't happen again."

Not wanting to see the look in her eyes, he pulled her into him, his hand cradling her head as he held her to his chest. When she let out a shuddering sigh of relief, he silently vowed to protect her for life. All he had to do was convince her that she didn't need protection from him.

THE DARKNESS ENGULFED THEM, but Sky had never felt more exposed. With the blanket over her, just her nose and mouth stuck out. She couldn't see where they were going and had to trust the man behind the wheel to get her to safety. But then, she did trust him, or she wouldn't have called him, right? The truth came down to one thing, she realized. She trusted him with her life but not her heart. Call it a preemptive strike by not putting herself in the position to watch Reece walk away when he experienced how hard her life was. That would be easier than believing for a heartbeat that they could be more than old friends.

The way he'd held her earlier before they left the safe house told her that much. He was strong but gentle. Comforting but honest. He didn't dismiss her fears by telling her everything would be okay—an empty promise in this situation. Everything might not be okay, but he would be there to make sure she was physically safe. She'd accepted that she might have to start over with her career even though the very idea made her sick. She had worked so hard for so long to prove herself as an artist, but now, one man was systematically dismantling her work. If even one gallery owner decided she was guilty, trial or no trial, she might as well hang up her easel and find a new career.

"Hanging in there?" Reece asked, his mouth covered with his arm as though he were coughing. He had told her he couldn't talk to her, or it would be obvious he wasn't alone.

"Yes, but it's not easy in this position," she admitted. "How much farther?"

"Ten," he grunted as though coughing again.

Ten minutes or ten miles, she didn't know, but she could hang on that long if it meant they'd get to safety. The last thing she wanted was Reece to get hurt in all this mess—bodily or professionally. In her opinion, it was above and beyond for Mina to bring them to Secure Watch, but maybe that was how they did business. Skylar knew she could never repay them, but she vowed to try.

"When this is over, I'm going to talk to my parents and the lawyer about getting an advance from my settlement to pay Secure Watch," she said, knowing he couldn't respond. "I can't say I don't have the money when I do."

As expected, he said nothing but dropped his hand from the wheel and squeezed her shoulder, telling her without words that he had things to say about it. They rode in silence for what seemed like forever to her, his hand still on her and his breathing steady, though she knew he was wound tight and on watch for the slightest thing to be off. All she wanted to do was get to Secure Watch, find a comfortable position for the first time in days and fall asleep. Her body was starting to feel the effects of the last forty-eight hours. If she wasn't careful, she was going to require more medical attention than they could give her.

"You will not take money from your settlement account to pay Secure Watch," he said, his words clipped.

"That's what the money is for, Reece. To take care of my expenses."

"Your medical and daily living expenses,

not this," he said, squeezing her shoulder. "If Secure Watch didn't want to help you, they wouldn't be, so please, don't insult everyone who is by insisting on paying."

"I'm disabled, not a charity case, Land," she said, anger rising in her chest.

"Did you hear me say you were?" he asked. Skylar couldn't see his face, but she could hear his exasperation loud and clear. Rather than distract him further, she sighed.

"Fine, I'll graciously accept the help of all of you at Secure Watch without bringing up payment. That said, you can't stop me from creating a special mosaic as a gift." She stressed the word *gift* so he didn't get his undies in a bundle about it.

Laughter rang out, making her smile, even though she didn't want to. "I certainly can't stop you from doing that, nor would I. Having a one-of-a-kind Skylar Sullivan mosaic is worth more than cash."

This time, Skylar's laughter filled the cab. "Land, you're smooth, but not smooth enough to make me forget that my name is mud right now in the art community, not that it was all that great to begin with. I was making gains, but now..." She didn't finish—she just shook her head under the blanket.

"Now, you'll come back stronger than ever

once the real culprit of the gallery crimes is caught and revealed. You'll be hailed as the hero for helping apprehend and bring them to justice."

"By hiding out in a cabin in the woods?"

"It's all about the spin, Sky. Spin it right and not only does this not hurt your career, but it also helps it."

"That would send this Binate guy right over the edge."

"I like to aim high," he said, and she could picture that one gray eye of his winking the way he used to do when they were kids. "There's a rest stop ahead. There aren't any headlights behind me, so I'll pull over and help you get upright and better secured for the rest of the ride. We're driving into heavy deer country, and I don't want you to get hurt if I have to hit the brakes."

"You won't hear me argue. Another ten minutes and I won't be able to sit up."

"Why didn't you say something sooner?" She heard the anger in his words, which was another reminder that he didn't live in her world and never would.

"To what end, Reece? Getting out alive but sore was better than getting out dead in a body bag. Don't judge me when you haven't been a part of my life for years. I'm tougher than you think I am."

"You're right. I haven't been part of your life for years, but whose fault is that?" he asked softly. She suspected he didn't want her to hear the question at all, but she had, and it made her grimace internally. Before she could respond, the truck slowed and they took a turn to the right, rolling her gently into his side to remind her that she would never enjoy the comfort of his warm body ever again.

He left the truck idling when he got out and slammed the door. *Slammed* was the apt description, but she was too busy trying to throw the blanket off to worry about his mood. The faster she got upright, the better for her body and their mission. Lingering in one spot wasn't a good idea, and she wouldn't be the reason for it.

By the time Reece had her door open, his gentleness had returned. "Take it slow," he said, offering his hand for her to grab with one hand while she pushed herself up with the other.

Bright lights filled the truck as a vehicle came down the exit, illuminating Reece where he stood at the passenger door. Reece ducked as she heard a pop and then the sound of pinging metal.

"Stay down!" he yelled, dropping her hand, yanking his handgun from its holster and firing off a shot.

Chapter Twelve

"Where the hell did these guys come from?" Reece yelled as he aimed for the tires on the truck as it passed them. They'd drilled the back of his truck full of holes, and he owed them one. On a breath, he squeezed the trigger, the bullet finding its target and blowing apart the giant tire of the lifted truck. The operator lost control immediately. Before he could get off another shot, the truck went careening into the grass until it bounced off several trees and rolled, landing on its roof with the tires still spinning.

"Let's go!" Reece slammed the door and ran to the driver's side, throwing the truck into Reverse and slamming the pedal down as far as it would go, praying none of the bullets had hit any of his tires or the gas tank. The engine roared under him, but the gas gauge didn't budge, nor did the truck fishtail. His truck might now be ugly, but at least it would get them to Secure Watch.

"Reece! What if that was Binate? Shouldn't we check?"

He briefly cut his gaze to hers once they were on the road again. "I let my guard down again with you and look what happened. There isn't a chance in hell I'm doing it again by approaching that truck. That leaves you open and defenseless, which is all Binate needs to grab you. I'm not stopping this truck again, so push yourself up using my shoulder and buckle in. Use my arm if you need extra leverage." He held his arm out in a V for her to grab, and after a few attempts, she managed to get herself upright and belted in. Rather than belt her legs together, she leaned over and wrapped her arms over them to hold them.

"You can't ride that way for the next hour," he said, glancing at her.

"The way you're driving, we'll be there in ten minutes."

Her words made him laugh, and he eased off the gas a bit. "I don't know about you, but I wouldn't mind picking up a cop right about now. In the absence of an escort, I'll push this truck to its limit if it means less time on the road alone. I need to update Secure Watch."

He went through every second of their drive in his mind, from leaving the safe house until they took that exit. No one was in the rearview mirror, especially not a truck that big. Where had they come from?

"That truck came from the wrong direction, Land," she said, turning to look at him. "It came down the on-ramp."

Reece blinked, forcing his mind away from the bullets to the moment the headlights filled the truck. He let out a breath. "You're right, but how did they know we left?"

"I can't answer that, since we left the bag and the tracker at the house."

Frustrated, he used voice controls to contact Mina.

"Secure Watch, Whiskey."

"Secure Watch, Riker," he addressed his boss. "There's been a situation."

"This seems to be the theme of our calls lately. I can't say I like it," Mina responded. "Is anyone hurt?"

"Negative," he answered, glancing at Sky, who looked like she'd fallen asleep on her legs. The position was uncomfortable, but he suspected she was scared and didn't want to be visible in the windows. Honestly, that wasn't an unfounded fear. "A jacked-up truck tried to take us out at the rest stop on 371."

"I like the use of the word *tried*."

"They're upside down in the grass with only three tires. My truck is full of holes, but otherwise, it's fine. I didn't wait around to see if it was Binate. I couldn't leave Sky unprotected."

"You did the right thing," she agreed. "Why were you at the rest stop? You didn't leave too long ago."

"Sky needed to sit up. She can't lie in certain positions for long or she starts to cramp up. Mina, when I tell you there was no one around us, I'm positive of that. The headlights were insane on the thing when it roared at us. Sky realized they came down the on-ramp."

"They had to be watching the house. It wouldn't take long for them to figure out where you were going and set up a trap."

"That or I do have a tracker on my truck. I checked it before we left again and found nothing, but I suppose they could have hacked the GPS in the maps."

"Impossible," she said immediately. "I have full control of that. I'm inclined to believe that whoever this Binate guy is, he has friends who are willing to help him. In this case, they could kill two birds with one stone."

"Take me out and grab Sky?"

"Yep," she answered grimly. "You made the right decision. How far out are you now?"

"Sky says at the speed I'm going, less than ten minutes." His words dragged a laugh from his boss. "About an hour. Sky is a mess, though—physically, I mean."

"Get her here in one piece. The cabin has a nice accessible shower. She can soak in some hot water and then get some sleep. We can pick this nonsense up tomorrow. In the meantime, I'll send a team of guys out to the rest stop on 371 and see what's left, if anything."

"I'm sure the guys will be long gone. That truck is going to take some work to get out of there, though."

"That's what I'm hoping," she agreed with a snicker. "If our guys can take a gander through it, we might be able to track down a registration. Call if you need more backup."

"Will do. Riker, out."

He punched the speaker off and eyed his passenger again. Knowing she couldn't stay like that the rest of the ride, he pulled the truck to the side of the road and kept his foot on the brake while he helped her roll over onto the bench seat, using his lap as a pillow. He lifted her legs onto the seat and tucked the seat belt around them so she could rest on her back instead of her side. It wasn't perfect, but as he pushed the speedometer toward one hundred miles per hour, he hoped to cut thirty minutes off the drive.

Once they were on the road again, she snuggled her head into his thigh, dangerously close to his groin, and sighed. He might have made a mess of this night, but she was safe and under his protection. That was all he cared about. After the little stunt they'd just pulled, Reece vowed to be the one to take Binate down.

SKY WOKE SLOWLY, her tired mind needing a moment to remember where she was until she glanced to her left and saw the man who still haunted her dreams. Last night, when they arrived at Secure One, the team had a UTV waiting to take them to their cabin near the lake. It was dark, so she couldn't see much as they meandered their way to the back of the property, but something told her the view would be spectacular when the sun came up. She did notice the room was lightening, which meant another day had arrived. A day that they would begin with a meeting of the Secure Watch team at breakfast, according to Reece.

One thing Skylar had noticed last night was that the property was a fortress in itself. You weren't escaping their security measures unless someone could scale a fence while invisible. Appropriate since Secure One was a security company. Reece had explained the harrowing story of Mina's kidnapping from the compound when she arrived years ago and how Cal, the owner of Secure One, and her husband's brother, took it as a personal affront. Since then, he's ensured no one could attack him in his home again. Short of someone dropping something from a plane, no one was getting inside without an invite. Since Secure One and Secure Watch worked together under the same roof, it was nice to be in the one place that could get her out of this jam. She once again found herself grateful for the invite.

Once they were in the cabin, Reece had encouraged her to sit under the hot water to ease some of the tension in her back so she could get some sleep. She'd never been more grateful than to find the cabin had enough modifications to keep her independent even during the worst time of her life. The shower was a roll-in with a shower wheelchair, something she didn't have the luxury of at home. Once she'd showered and gotten ready for bed, she'd tried to convince Reece to let her sleep in the recliner so he could have the bed, but it had been a losing battle. He already had the bed set up and ready for her when she came out of the bathroom, including a heating pad for her back. Then he'd sat next to her and rubbed her forehead silently until she'd dropped off to sleep. To say she was surprised to see him in bed next to her wasn't true. There was no other option other than the recliner, but Land would defend her until his death, and there was no way he'd leave her vulnerable, even on a property that was monitored from all angles by his colleagues.

Reece wasn't wired that way. It was all or nothing for this man, and she had always loved that about him when they were kids. He never did anything halfway and didn't let anyone else get away with doing a job halfway, either. The Land-sized gulf she'd had inside her for the last fourteen years deepened, and a tear ran from her eye.

"Hey," he whispered, wiping it away gently. "Talk to me."

That was the last thing she was going to do. Opening up about that gulf of pain she carried regarding him would change their dynamics, and they couldn't afford to be anything but objective right now. It would be too easy for her to lose sight of why she'd pushed him away all those years ago.

"I refuse to drag you into this dumpster fire of my life," she whispered. When he lifted a brow, she sighed. "Okay, drag you any deeper into this dumpster fire I call life."

"I'm in it to win it, Sky," he promised, running his knuckle down her cheek to catch another tear. "A few tears won't scare me away if that's what you think."

"Tears never scared you away, Land."

"Sometimes they drove me to do stupid things, but I always came back," he said with a wink.

Until the time he didn't. She'd wanted it that way, though. She'd begged him to stay away from her and to get on with his life. When he had, she'd died inside, knowing she would never get to see him achieve all his dreams. They'd shared so much during their childhood, but it wasn't fair to hold him back when he could make his dreams come true.

"We're in the right place now to sort all of this out," he promised, brushing her hair off her forehead. "I have every tool at my disposal, and now that I don't have to worry about keeping you safe while trying to do my job, I hope we can resolve this even more quickly."

"That's good. The sooner I'm out of your hair, the better," she agreed, prepared to sit up and get the day started, but he grabbed her elbow and held her there.

"First, you aren't 'in my hair,'" he said, using air quotes with one hand. "I'm here because I want to be. Second, things aren't going to go back to the way they were before, Sky. I won't allow it."

Her heart hammered in her chest as he forced eye contact. His eyes told her everything he meant by that statement, but like a moth to a flame, she had to ask. "Back to the way they were before?"

"Both of us pretending the other doesn't exist," he said, his gaze holding hers. "There's no way I can go back to that way of life, so once we solve this problem, we're going to be friends again—the kind of friends who see each other and spend time together."

"No, Land—"

Before she could say more, his lips brushed hers. Sound and light disappeared when he did it again, this time letting his lips linger on hers. His warm breath met hers and she whimpered, wanting more but also afraid to want more. He solved that problem for her by pressing his lips to hers fully and sliding his fingers into her hair, holding her there as they breathed together in harmony for a split second. When he pulled back, he ran his thumb across her lips.

"It looks like it's time to start the day," he whispered, his thumb still grazing her overly sensitive skin. "The team will be waiting for us. Give me five minutes to clean up, and then the bathroom will be all yours."

Slowly, he pulled his fingers from her hair without breaking eye contact. The things she read in his eyes were dangerous to her way of life if she allowed him to touch her again. When he tossed the blanket off and climbed from the bed, her gaze followed him to the bathroom, his joggers low on his hips and his hard, muscular chest bare with just a smattering of blond hair. He was just as sculpted as in high school, but maturity looked good on him.

The moment the bathroom door clicked shut, she brought her hand to her lips. She'd been kissed before, but not like that. Not by someone's entire heart. And that was the only way she could describe it. It might have been the tamest kiss in history, but the action wasn't the point. The underlying emotions were the point. Hurt. Anger. Pain. Loss. Joy. Desire. Trust. She felt them all, and each one had pierced her heart and lodged there as an arrowed reminder of their past and why they couldn't have a future.

BREAKFAST HAD BEEN DELICIOUS. Reece had told her that their cook, Sadie, made a huge breakfast and dinner every night for the entire crew, which had to be a massive undertaking, from what Sky could see. Only part of the crew had been there, but the cafeteria was still full. According to Mina, Secure One and Secure Watch had more than doubled in size since she moved there with her husband, Roman. That wasn't even counting their remote operatives like Reece. She was starting to see the scope of who was helping her and how much power they had to make sure she rolled out of this alive. After last night, she didn't even care if she had a career to return to as long as she and Reece were still breathing at the end. As far as she was concerned, that was all that mattered anymore.

"You didn't eat much for breakfast," Reece said as they rolled into the conference room to decide the next move on the board. They didn't have many, but she had confidence that Mina had mapped them all and knew exactly what percentage each one had of working.

"I have a bit of a headache," she answered as he pulled a chair away from the large conference table so she could park her chair under it. Once her wheels were locked, she shifted in the chair to find a more comfortable position. The truth was, the ride to Secure Watch last night had left lasting effects. Her belly hurt from being hunched over for so long, but she wouldn't complain since she was alive to see the sunrise this morning. "I'll grab a snack later."

Once they were settled, Mina leaned in on the table. "I'm not going to lie—this has been a challenge. Binate knows what he's doing when it comes to hiding his footprints and your information. It's hard to stump me, but he's thwarted my every move."

"Mine as well," Reece agreed.

"That's why it's not Silas," Sky said, shaking her head. "He doesn't have the skill set to do this."

"He didn't when he left home, but that was nearly fifteen years ago," Mina gently said. "People change."

"Especially when driven by hatred or desire for revenge," Reece added.

Skylar adjusted herself in the chair again, partly to get more comfortable and partly to avoid spouting off at him about her brother. "I know you think I'm hindered by family alliance when it comes to Silas, but I'm not. I don't disagree that people change, but what you don't know is that Silas was diagnosed with schizophrenia when he was—"

"Nineteen," Reece finished before she could. "Why didn't you tell me?"

"My parents were adamant no one know," Sky said, averting her gaze from him and Mina.

"I'm lost," Mina said.

"When Sky was thirteen, I walked in on Silas attempting to assault her. Silas was nineteen at the time."

Mina's lips thinned. "My guess is that didn't go well."

"My brother was a waif," Skylar said. "Reece was bigger in height and weight, even six years younger. After Silas got out of the ER, my parents put him into therapy, where he was eventually diagnosed through a psychiatrist. Mom and Dad tried to help him, but—"

"You can't help someone who doesn't want help," Mina finished, and Sky pointed at her as if to say, *Exactly.* "All that said, I'm still following him as a lead, but I'm also looking closely at Miles Bradshaw. His past tells me he's an angry man. What I don't know yet is if he's capable of such a sophisticated wipe of someone's life."

Skylar braced her elbow on the table and rested her head on her hand as Mina and Reece tossed ideas back and forth. She couldn't pretend she hadn't noticed the hurt in Reece's eyes when he learned of Silas's diagnosis, but it also hadn't been her choice not to tell him. She'd wanted to, but her mom said if she told Reece, he'd tell his parents. For a reason she wasn't privy to, they didn't want anyone else to know of Silas's problems. Maybe it was time to let that ghost out of the closet and bury it once and for all.

Mina and Reece were deep in conversation, but she needed to use the restroom. "I'll be right back," she said, pointing out the door. "I just need the facilities."

"Need help?" Reece asked, pausing their conversation, but she shook her head.

"I'm fine. Thanks, though."

Before he could say more, she wheeled out of the room and down the hallway toward the cafeteria. She had noticed a restroom on their way to the conference room. Once locked inside, she pulled her shirt up and uncoiled her catheter. She wondered if her bladder was full, which would explain her pain. Once she had it uncoiled and over the bowl, she uncapped it, but nothing happened.

There was a knock on the door. "Sky, are you okay?" Reece asked.

"No. I think I need help," she said without thinking, her head pounding as she tried to recap the catheter. Before she could coil it, the lock popped and Reece held the door open for a woman she didn't know, then followed her into the small space.

"My name is Selina. I'm the crew nurse," she explained, kneeling in front of her chair.

"I didn't think you looked right when you left," Reece explained.

Selina was already checking her pulse before Reece finished speaking. "Does your head hurt?"

"Yes. I can't even remember how to get the catheter to flow, but my stomach hurts," Skylar admitted.

"Med bay, now," Selina said to Reece, who scooped her from the chair and ran down the hallway. "I'm worried it's autonomic dysreflexia."

"That's bad, right?" Reece asked as he laid her on a stretcher in a room that could have been an emergency room cubicle. "I remember that was a worry when you first were injured."

"It's always a worry," Selina explained, hooking her to the blood pressure machine by the bed. "There are many reasons someone with a spinal cord injury can develop autonomic dysreflexia, but when it happens, it's hazardous to the heart."

Snapping on gloves, Selina checked around her catheter and palpated her abdomen. "Your bladder is very full, so now we know the culprit," she said, grabbing a urinal. "You don't free drain?"

"Only at night. Intermittent draining is normally not a problem, but I'm worried the positioning in the truck last night damaged something."

"She was bent over for quite a while," Reece explained, taking hold of her hand. She was too scared to pull away from him. The warmth of his skin grounded her and made her feel like she would be okay.

Selina glanced up at the monitor when the blood pressure cuff deflated. "Blood pressure is high, but not in the immediate danger zone. I vote to change the catheter rather than try to make this one drain. Are you okay with that?"

"You can do that here?"

Reece chuckled, though she could tell it was forced. "She could do open-heart surgery here if she had to."

"I wouldn't go that far," Selina said, snapping on gloves. "As for a catheter, that's a piece of cake. I need to lay you flat, so tell me if your headache worsens when I do that. We will change it fast, drain your bladder and then reassess your blood pressure."

"Will that fix it?" Reece asked as she gathered supplies.

"If we can't keep the urine flowing, then we'll need to do something else with the catheter or get her to a hospital. If we're lucky, it's just sediment blocking this one and a new tube will solve the issue. I want you at her head to call out the blood pressure numbers each time it deflates. Keep an eye on her skin. Tell me if she starts sweating or her face gets red and blotchy."

"It's just a headache right now," Skylar assured them. "And I'm a little warm."

Selina paused and offered her a smile as she pulled the gloves off and squeezed her hand. "I've got you. Where's your level of injury?"

"T5," Reece answered before she could.

"I can't feel my bladder at all," Skylar added. Selina nodded as she lowered the bed and immediately snapped on new gloves.

Reece held her face in his hands and her gaze with his. "You'll be okay. Selina is the best there is," he promised, dropping a kiss on her forehead. "She's right. She's warm."

"That's not unexpected, but watch for excessive sweating," Selina answered as she worked. In less than a minute, she heard the catheter start draining into the urinal.

"That was crazy fast," Skylar said, a laugh escaping before she coughed once. "It takes me ten minutes to change that catheter."

"Selina can remove a bullet while riding a skateboard," Reece said with a wink. "How's your head?"

"Still hurts, but the pounding has slowed."

"That's because your bladder is almost empty," Selina said. "Did you empty it this morning?"

"Of course," she answered defensively. "Only

a small amount came out, but we went to bed late, so I didn't think too much of it."

"There was no way you could in that case," Selina agreed. "Reece, what are the blood pressure numbers?"

Reece turned his head, giving her a side profile that made her want to weep. He was so handsome. She'd never seen a man with blond facial hair, which made him look like a Norske hunter. "One forty over eighty."

Selina nodded. "Good, it's coming down."

"Isn't that normal?" Reece asked, turning his attention back to her.

"For someone without a spinal cord injury, yes. I would guess Skylar's runs lower than that."

"By a lot," she agreed. "I'd like to see if it keeps coming down before I take medication, though. That usually makes it drop too much."

"We can do that," Selina agreed. "I'm going to sit you up now, which will help, too. Then, we'll decide how best to approach the catheter situation. Reece, would you go down and update the team?"

"No, I don't want to leave her." He shook his head, refusing to look away from her long enough to address his friend.

Selina walked to the head of the bed and put her hand on his shoulder. "I know you don't, but I'll need to monitor her for a few hours. You can check on her, but those are hours wasted and you could be helping Mina sort this out so Skylar can get her life back. You can trust her with me."

"I trust you, Selina. But I—"

"I know," she promised with a wink, stopping him from saying whatever he planned to say. "Trust me with her for a little bit. She'll be all the better for it."

He glanced down and met her gaze. "Are you okay with me leaving? If you aren't, say the word."

"She's right," she said with a nod. "There's no sense in wasting time with me when you could be helping Mina."

"Being here with you is not wasting time," he said as she brushed her hand across his face. His beard was soft and smooth against her palm. Tears pricked her eyes when she thought about the life with this man she'd been forced to give up.

"I promise to call you if there's even a hint of a problem," Selina said when she moved to the head of the stretcher. "You go do what you do best and I'll do what I do best. Okay?"

Reece made eye contact with Selina momentarily before glancing down at her again. "I'd be mad, but I'm too relieved that you're okay.

I'll chat with Mina for a few minutes and then check on you."

"I can live with that," she whispered when she realized how truly terrified he was about what had happened. That was when she remembered this was the reason she'd let him go the first time.

Chapter Thirteen

The memories overwhelmed Reece until he fell backward and slid down the wall, his head in his hands and his breathing ragged in the quiet space. He squeezed his eyes shut to try and push the memories away, but it didn't work.

"My legs! I can't feel my legs!" Sky cried, terror ripping through him as he knelt on the turf next to her.

"Help is coming," Reece promised, holding her hand as tears streamed down her face. "Don't move."

"I can't move." She didn't scream or cry those three words. Instead, they were barely a whisper, as though the realization had dawned on her that life as they knew it was over.

"Riker!" The sharp tone snapped his head up, and he came face-to-face with Roman. He held his hand out until Reece took it and let Roman help him up. "You look like a man who needs a cup of coffee," he said.

Roman led him down to the cafeteria where Sadie kept hot, fresh coffee going 24-7. He poured them each a cup before they sat at a table to drink it.

"Thanks," Reece said, holding up the cup. "It's been a long few days."

"Filled with many tense, destructive memories," Roman added. "I remember how hard it was not to be overwhelmed by the emotions when I saw Mina for the first time after searching for her for a year. To see how much pain they're in does something to you here," he said, pounding his chest.

"My problem seems to be here," Reece said, pointing at his head. "Always has been since the accident."

"I know what happened to Skylar from helping Mina on the case, but now I understand that the accident affected you far more than a broken wrist."

"It was my fault," Reece said, lowering the cup to the table. "It was the final routine for the event and we thought we had the first-place podium clinched, so we decided to do an easier stunt lift than we'd planned. There was no point in risking the medal by trying something too hard. The stunt was flawless until I found myself on the ground and Sky ten feet away, unable to move."

Roman sipped his coffee silently while Reece slumped over his coffee mug. "I'm still waiting to hear how it's your fault."

"I didn't catch her!" he exclaimed. "It's not hard, man."

Reece noticed Roman blink several times and then opened and closed his mouth twice. "How were you supposed to catch her when you'd been plowed over by a golf cart and had a broken arm?"

"With the other one," Reece growled.

Roman leaned over the table and folded his hands. "Listen, Reece. I've been where you are multiple times while serving in the army. I blamed myself for something I had no control over. Then I worked with Mina for eight years, and on that final day, I let her down. I wasn't there when she needed me. She was injured and suffered needlessly for an entire year because of my impotence. I've learned from my brothers here that it's normal to feel that way, especially when it's about the woman you love."

"Roman, no," he said with a shake of his head. "It's not like that. We were childhood best friends, that's it."

"Oh, yeah, that's totally what I see in front of me right now. A man worried about his childhood best friend."

Reece rolled his eyes. He couldn't stop it if he

tried, because he had no defense when it came to Sky—never had.

"Is Skylar okay?" Roman asked when the silence stretched on.

"She will be, according to Selina. Her catheter was kinked and not draining, causing a dangerous elevation of her blood pressure. That was my fault, too. She had to ride in an awkward position last night after everything that happened. I should have thought of having Selina check her over when we arrived."

"Was Skylar concerned about it?"

"No. Sky told Selina that it was draining this morning. She just didn't realize it wasn't emptying fully."

"Then I don't think you can blame yourself for something Skylar controls. All you can do is get her help when she needs it and be there to support her. It seems to me that's exactly what you're doing."

"It's not enough, man," Reece said, shaking his head. "I'll spend the rest of my life knowing I didn't save her that night. That's why she pushed me away after high school."

"Are you sure about that, son?" Cal asked as he walked through the door.

"Hey, Cal. Sorry about the drama. I'll get back to work here." Anything to get away from these two men who were mentors, friends and wise beyond their years. He enjoyed nothing more than talking with them, but not when it was about *his* life.

"I'm not your boss, son. You don't have to apologize to me. Besides, the last time I checked, you've been doing your job 24-7 for the last few days. Take a break and a breath, or you'll be no good to anyone, especially the woman who needs you the most."

Roman motioned at him with his hand while nodding. "Exactly what I've been trying to tell him."

"Secure One, Sierra," they heard over Cal's walkie-talkie, and he grabbed it, pressing the button. "Secure two, Charlie."

"Let Reece know that Skylar's blood pressure is normal again and her headache has resolved. I need to keep her for at least another hour, but she's out of the woods."

Cal pushed the button and held it out for Reece to answer. "Thanks, Selina. I appreciate everything you do."

"Oh, hey, Reece. It's no problem. Skylar is napping now that everything has been resolved. The exhaustion isn't helping the situation, so I want to let her rest for as long as possible. Can you work without her?"

Cal handed him the device and, taking possession of the cold plastic box, straightened Reece's spine a notch. "Yes, and I'd prefer it that way. The less stress she's under, the better. Do you agree?"

"From a medical standpoint, absolutely. This is stressful, but if she can get some rest, she may be able to cope with it better."

"Ten-four," Reece said. "Keep me posted, but I'll stop in after I check with Mina."

"She's in good hands, Reece," Selina said, her voice dropping slightly. "I know you want to be her hero, and you are, from what she tells me, so just take a deep breath and do what you do best while I do what I do best. Okay?"

"Can do, Selina. Thank you." Reece handed the walkie back to Cal and stood from the table. It was time to do what he did best and resolve this situation so he could put Skylar out of his mind again. Any idea that they could be together ended when he remembered he wasn't her hero. He was her nightmare.

WHEN SKYLAR WOKE, she buried her face in the pillow so she didn't have to face Selina immediately. All she could see was the look on Land's face when he'd carried her to the med bay and then the lancing guilt when he'd spotted the catheter. She moaned and regretted it instantly, as Selina was by her side before it ended.

"You're awake. How are you feeling?"

"Awful," she moaned, throwing her arm over her forehead to block the light from her eyes. "How did I let this happen?"

"You didn't let anything happen," Selina gently reminded her. "Life just happens sometimes. You've been under severe stress and unusual conditions that your body isn't used to. You have to expect a few hiccups along the way."

"I'm not talking about that," she whispered.

"You mean Reece." Her nod was enough of an answer. "I've kept him updated, and he's been down to check on you a few times. He's been working with Mina on your case."

Rather than try to explain further, Skylar just nodded as though that was the end of it. "How is the catheter draining now?"

"Excellent," Selina answered. "I'm going to change it again before you leave, though. If there was any sediment in your bladder from it being so full, I want to make sure we clear it out and then put in a new catheter. That's why I've been free draining it for the last few hours."

"Do you think I can go back to intermittent drainage? A bag is going to be extremely inconvenient right now." *Not to mention embarrassing*, she thought.

"During the day? No problem. I would still free drain it at night."

"I always do," Skylar said. "Well, I always

do at home. Lately, sleep has been few and far between."

"That's easy to understand. Hopefully now that you're here, you can rest better at night, which will help your body deal better during the day."

Selina gathered the supplies needed to change the catheter while Skylar looked around the med bay. "This place is intense for a private medical suite. Are you a doctor or something?"

"Or something," she said with a smile. "I'm an ex-cop turned search and rescue paramedic turned advanced practice paramedic when I had to start over in life. Cal hired me as an operative and paramedic, but I found my place here in the med bay. I do certain ops with the guys when they need a medical person and an extra agent, but after much self-reflection, I realized that my favorite thing to do is help people. That's when I decided to play to my strengths."

"It sounds like you've lived an interesting life," Skylar said with a smile. "I'm lucky you decided to play to your strengths, or I'd be dead."

Selina smiled as she snapped on gloves and started changing the catheter. "I'm lucky to do what I love with the person I love."

"Oh, your significant other works here, too?"

"Yep. My husband, Efren. He was a sharp-shooter for the army and then worked as a bodyguard, which is how he came to work here for Secure One. Now, he's an operative on the security team. He's an above-knee amputee."

"Oh," Skylar said, not making eye contact. After all the years of dealing with medical professionals, she was used to letting others take control of her body. She didn't like it, but she'd learned that it wasn't always worth fighting for independence regarding her health. Sure, she could change the catheter herself, but it was more difficult for her to do it. Allowing Selina to do the task meant the catheter wouldn't give her any more problems, which was crucial in her current situation.

"All done," Selina said, attaching the new catheter to the drain bag. "I'll let it drain until you're ready to go and then I'll cap it off and you can take control of it again. Reece brought your chair down and said he'd help you transfer when you were ready."

The sigh escaped before she could stop it, so she looked away from the woman who had been nothing but kind to her. "Maybe I'll just stay here forever."

Selina's laughter was soft as she walked back to the stretcher. "That never seems to be a good way to deal with our problems."

But Reece was a problem Skylar didn't know how to deal with.

"Maybe not." She wanted to say more, but she couldn't promise that if she did, she would be able to hold back the tears.

Selina took her hand and held it, offering a smile of understanding. "You're overwhelmed, tired, scared and angry. That's all understandable. When you toss in medical situations like you deal with, it's easier to pretend none of it is happening than face it head-on. There isn't a person in this building who doesn't understand that. You're among friends here. We want to help."

"I've never been more grateful," Skylar said, a shaky smile tipping her lips.

"But that's also part of the problem, right?" Selina asked, and Skylar tipped her head in confusion. "Reece."

"Oh." That was all she said, because saying anything more would have ended in tears. Once she started crying, she wasn't sure she could stop.

"He's really worried about you. Roman and Cal had to talk him down off the ledge after he left you here."

"He's always been my defender," she agreed, still not making eye contact. "He feels guilty for what happened to me, even though it wasn't his fault."

"There isn't a person in this building who doesn't understand that, too. We also understand pushing people away because we think it's in their best interest."

"It is," she assured the woman. "Now he knows it, too. If there's one thing this episode did, it taught him what my life is like and why he doesn't want to be part of it."

"But what if he does?"

Skylar shook her head wildly. "He doesn't. Not after what he saw today. The accident hasn't been kind."

"You're upset that he saw your stoma?"

"I'm upset that he saw it all," she whispered. "My para-belly, the stoma, my body's reaction to the situation." She shook her head against the pillow. "It doesn't matter. It doesn't matter."

"It feels kind of like it matters, Skylar. You're a woman. Understandably, you don't want your crush to see you like this."

"He's not my crush." The words were vehement even if they weren't true. "I didn't want him to see it because he'd just feel worse about the accident. It's bad enough I had to call him and ask for help. I knew he'd do it out of guilt, but I had nowhere else to turn."

"He's not helping you out of guilt, Skylar.

He's helping you because he cares about you, whether you like it or not. Honestly, that's his right. You're a beautiful woman, para-belly, stoma and all. You can't blame him for being attracted to you."

"He's not. We're old friends in a strange situation."

"Okay, well, let's just say your para-belly and stoma are the least important part of who you are and Reece knows that. I'm not a therapist or a psychiatrist, but I do recommend that you talk to him about what happened. Be honest with him about how you're feeling so he can be honest about the same."

Selina patted her hand and then released it to take her blood pressure again. Skylar closed her eyes, but all she could see was the look of concern on his face. That was when she realized he had never taken his eyes off hers. Maybe he hadn't seen as much as she thought or didn't register it if he had. Did it matter? No. He should see it all. Let him see her sagging belly and the tube doing what she no longer could. Maybe it was the reality check he needed after that kiss this morning. She would cherish it forever as the one and only kiss she'd get from the only man she would ever love. That didn't mean she wanted him to stay with her. It meant that she loved him enough to let him go.

Chapter Fourteen

Mina walked into the conference room with her lips in a thin line. Cal and Iris Knowles followed her into the room. Iris was a member of the Secure Watch team and was second to none in her work, but she struggled with social situations, so Reece was surprised to see her here. He had no doubt what she was about to tell them was anything but good news.

The only good news he'd gotten today was when Selina called him an hour ago to say that Sky was ready to leave the med bay. He'd dropped what he was doing and run down there to help. Once she was back in her chair and he'd taken the information Selina had given him about what to watch for should the autonomic dysreflexia flare, they'd returned to the command center to work through the videos on her Facebook page. He wanted her to rest, but she insisted she was fine and wanted to resolve this sooner rather than later. He didn't blame her. He couldn't imagine what it must be like to be in her shoes and not know if she would get her life back. He'd worked with many people in the same situation during his career, but it was different when it was someone you were close to. He hated using the past tense when it came to Sky and prayed that he no longer had to when this was over. But the look on Mina's face told him they might be a step closer to answers.

"I have news," she said, setting the tablet down.

"It doesn't seem like good news, judging by the look on your face," Sky said from beside him. He smiled. She was never about mincing words.

"You could say that," Cal agreed, glancing at Mina. "We'll walk you through it."

Mina handed a sheet of paper to Reece. "An arrest warrant?" he asked, skimming it. "Wait. I don't understand. I thought the cops knew she didn't do this."

"That's what we thought as well," Cal said. "Then I heard from one of my contacts at the Duluth PD that they had no choice but to up-date the warrant and execute it."

"I'm confused," Skylar said. "How are they going to arrest someone who doesn't exist?"

"That's where things get interesting," Mina said, and Reece could see the wheels spinning in her head. She had found a thread to pull and was giddily unwinding it. "Skylar Sullivan once again exists in the world. Everything has been restored except for your social media pages. Binate is still controlling those."

"And your bank accounts have been restored but emptied," Cal added. Skylar gasped, but Cal held up his hand so he could finish. "Your accounts are protected, so we're gathering the proper information to send the bank so your balances can be restored once you're clear of this."

"And you think the sudden return to the living for Skylar Sullivan was for the purpose of the arrest warrant?" Reece asked Mina, who nodded.

"I believe that Binate finally forced their hand by causing damage to enough galleries that they didn't have a choice. Since Skylar is now 'missing—'" she added air quotes "—it looks like she ran."

"Pun not intended," Sky added, making his lips twitch.

"Rolled," Mina said, with the tip of her fake hat.

"It has to be Miles," Skylar said, her arms crossed over her chest in a tight embrace. "No one else I can think of would hate me enough to go through this much to set me up."

Reece could, and his name was Silas, but he knew better than to say it. Skylar was stressed enough, and tossing her brother into the mix wouldn't help matters. Instead, he gently tugged her arms off her chest and rested them on her lap. "Remember what Selina said about keeping your posture open and not tense for the rest of the day."

The scathing look she sent him would have made a weaker man cower. "Thank you, WebMD, for your insight into living in my body."

Mina snorted, and Reece sent her a glare that did nothing but make her grin wider.

"I'm still digging up dirt on Miles Bradshaw," Iris said, speaking for the first time. She stared at the table, not making eye contact with anyone, which wasn't unusual. She'd been in an accident as a child that left her with a traumatic brain injury. "He's a disgusting individual, I can tell you that." Iris finally looked up and met Sky's gaze for half a second before she dropped it again. "If there's a way to tie him to this, I'll find it."

"Thanks, Iris," Reece said with a smile, knowing she'd never see it but appreciating her nonetheless.

"No thanks needed. I'm doing the job that I'm paid to do." Cal cleared his throat, and Iris grimaced. "Sorry." She glanced at Sky again. "I had an accident when I was younger, too. It scrambled my brain and messed up the pathways that would have helped me in social situations. I apologize for my bluntness. It's not that I don't care. It's that I don't know how to show it."

"You're fine, Iris," Sky assured her. "I appreciate that you're here helping me. Honestly, bluntness is good, especially in this situation. Coddling isn't necessary when my life and livelihood are at stake."

Iris nodded once as though she agreed with everything Sky had said. "Miles Bradshaw is a boil on the backside of life," she said, jumping right back into the situation at hand.

"I couldn't have said that better myself," Sky agreed.

"I thought I was stunted socially, but this guy has zero filters and zero humility. If someone isn't stroking his ego and calling him pretty at all times, he takes it as a personal affront."

"It's like you've met him or something," Sky muttered. "Miles is all of those things."

"And more," Iris said, holding up her finger. "Turns out, he prides himself on being an aficionado when it comes to sussing out fake art."

"Spoiler alert," Sky said, "his art is the fake art."

"That is correct," she agreed. "Or, at the very least, it's copied art."

"Meaning?" Cal asked as he tried to follow the conversation.

"Meaning he may make the art, but he's using other artists' ideas. Maybe he changes the colors, but the designs are always a copy of someone else's work."

"Is this something I can have my police contact look at him for?" Cal asked, and Iris sat blinking at him in confusion.

"He means, is it something Miles can be arrested for," Reece clarified for her.

"Oh! No, I mean, not really. He changes it just enough to claim it's 'original,' even when the design is recycled. It's kind of like fan fiction. It resembles the original story, but they change it enough so it's not obvious plagiarism."

Sky motioned at Iris. "Exactly that. And it's not illegal to use someone else's design— it's just lazy. If you look through his portfolio, you understand why no one wants to carry his work in their galleries. The galleries and shops around Duluth are looking for unique pieces. Even when he can convince someone to take his work—that's usually due to a hard guilt he lays on them—the art doesn't sell and they sever ties with him quickly. He can't take constructive criticism, either. And not about his art, because art is in the eye of the beholder, but about his propensity to push people away rather than engage. Miles doesn't have a future in the art world as it stands now. Maybe if he came up with something original, he could move to a different city and find a place for it. First, he'd have to change his entire personality. I don't see that happening."

Cal leaned toward Sky and Iris. "Personal opinion time. Do you think Miles is capable of vandalizing these galleries?"

"Yes," they said in unison, lifting his lips into a smile.

"Most especially because of his hatred for Skylar," Iris said. "I found some posts on a public forum board that were anything but complimentary."

Sky rolled her eyes as Iris handed out some papers to everyone. "All I could do was sort through and find some of the best ones. There was a lot to choose from. Sorry, Skylar, but he doesn't like you."

Sky's laughter filled the room. It lifted Reece's heart and brought him back to life. If Sky was laughing, she was going to be okay.

"Sweetheart, that is not information I didn't already have. The last altercation we got into was in February. Long story short, he got mad when another art gallery dumped him."

"Tell them why," Reece encouraged her, wondering if this was the crux of the problem all along.

"I could prove that some of the art he sent them was manufactured."

The room was dead silent for a beat before Cal whistled. "That sounds like motive to me."

"He was so angry security had to remove him from the event, and the event planners banned him for the rest of time," Reece explained. "He claims that Sky's art is the problem because she uses recycled materials."

"That sounds like my kind of art," Iris said. "If I want manufactured pieces, I can go to the store. If I want unique, I'll look for an artist doing something unusual in the art form."

Sky nodded as she made eye contact with every person in the room. "I know who Miles Bradshaw is. This is not new, unexpected or distressing information. He was the first person I thought of when Mina told me to think of people who might have a beef with me. If he could make me go away without it blowing back on him, he would."

"Make you go away?" Cal asked with a lifted brow.

"He says I use my disability to get sympathy, which is why people buy my work."

"See line four," Iris said, shaking the paper.

Heads dipped as everyone read line four. Reece saw red. "'I'd like to drive that sorry excuse for an artist into Lake Superior. I'm so tired of her poor-pitiful-me routine at events. The only reason people buy her art is because they feel guilty that she uses a wheelchair.'"

"Wow," Mina said, lowering her own paper. "He really doesn't like you."

"Established," Sky said with an eye roll. "The thing is, I'm not sure he has the skills to do all of this."

"From what I can see, he doesn't," Iris agreed. "I'm still digging to see if he has friends who do."

"Miles has friends?" Skylar asked the question with such shock that Reece snorted.

"None I've found so far, but I'll keep looking."

Skylar froze and turned to Reece. "Camille Castillo."

"Who?" Mina asked, but Sky never took her eyes off Reece.

"Camille Castillo. They were tight, like two peas in a pod."

Reece noticed Mina patiently waiting for him to get the information for her and nodded. "Is Camille from Duluth, and is she as aggressive as Miles?"

"I don't know if she's from Duluth," Sky

answered, turning to the rest of the team as though she had just remembered they were there. "But she's been part of the art scene for…" She tossed her head back and forth as though trying to sort things out. "At least a year now. She's always the first to come to Miles's defense, but when asked if they're together, she vehemently denies it."

"So they're friends but not lovers?" Mina asked.

Sky gave her the palms up. "I can't answer that, but I know they're friends. Iris jogged my memory on that, so thank you." Iris gave her a nod before she stared at the table again. "I'm not her favorite person, either." Sky gave him a cheeky smile, and he couldn't help but laugh. "That said, I haven't had the same hostile interactions with her that I've had with Miles. Camille does stained-glass art that's gorgeous and all original. She sells well in all the galleries, so I haven't figured out why she hangs with Miles. Not that I've spent too much energy thinking about it."

"Camille Castillo." Mina spelled the name aloud, and Sky nodded when she finished. "Do you know her age?"

"Not her exact age, but she's close to mine. There can't be that many Camille Castillos in Duluth."

"Iris," Mina said, "I'll hand you this to look at since you're digging on Miles."

"Yes, boss," Iris said, scratching on her pad of paper.

"She probably has nothing to do with this," Sky said, glancing between everyone while chewing on her lip. "I just thought maybe you could learn more about Miles through her."

Reece gently rubbed her neck. "She won't know we're looking into her. This is purely information gathering."

"That's correct," Mina said with a reassuring smile. "If they're friends, maybe he's staying at her house or working together on a project. It's important to check out the people close to him so we can eliminate them as part of the problem. Now, that brings us to the videos. Did you find anything, Iris?"

Iris shook her head. "As you know, it's nearly impossible to reverse engineer a voice like the one Binate is using."

"I don't understand," Skylar said, glancing around the table. "Reverse engineer it?"

"They're trying to decipher Binate's voice to see if you can recognize it," Reece explained.

"I tried everything, but as expected, I couldn't hear the original voice," Iris replied.

"That's another thing," Skylar said. "The fact that he uses 'Binate' rather than 'Binary' is telling. Miles would never use something so overly used as 'Binary.' He'd find something close that means the same thing."

"Wow, he really stretched himself going with 'Binate,'" Iris said with an eye roll to which no one could hide their snort.

"That's Miles for ya," Skylar said.

"Well, I got this sound when I started playing with the recording. Do you recognize it?" Iris asked.

She held up her finger and then pressed a button on her computer. A sound filled the room, and Skylar glanced at Reece. "That's a ship's horn."

"A laker," Reece agreed. "He has to be somewhere by the lake to pick that up."

"Lakers honk going in and out of a harbor, right?" Cal asked.

"Yes, and occasionally if they pass another ship, but you'd be hard-pressed to hear that on the shore from the middle of a shipping lane, especially loud enough to be picked up on a recording."

"You're saying our best bet is to search areas around a harbor?" Mina asked, and Reece nodded.

"You can eliminate any harbor that can't accommodate the big lakers, but my bet would be on Duluth/Superior or Two Harbors. That said, I don't know how it helps."

"We'll look for any property owned by Miles or his family. If we find any, it's a place to investigate. In the meantime, I want you to take Skylar back to the cabin and comb through those videos," Mina said.

"What are we looking for?" Skylar asked.

"Anything that might give him away," she explained. "Something he might say that jogs your memory about a conversation you had with him or something you know about him. That kind of thing."

"I can do that," Skylar said with a nod. "Cal, will you get in trouble if the police find out I'm here? Or do they already know?"

"No and no," Cal said. "If they learn you're here, they'd need a warrant to enter the property. That said, there's no way they'll find out you're here. We all know you aren't responsible for the vandalizations. Even my cop friend knows that, but they're being pressured to find you."

"I can understand that," Skylar said, shaking her head sadly. "I'm just upset that anyone thinks I'd ever damage anything, much less an art gallery."

"What matters is that none of us here believe it," Reece said, squeezing her hand gently.

"What he said," Mina agreed. "Not only would it be physically impossible, but it doesn't make sense. Whoever thought this up isn't the brightest bulb in the pack."

"Miles." Iris coughed the word, bringing a smile to Reece's lips.

"I hate to agree with her, but I do," Skylar said. "As long as no one is going to get in trouble for me being here, we'll watch those videos repeatedly if it helps you guys figure this out."

"You're safe here," Cal said, squeezing her shoulder. "Considering the day you've had, I don't want you to worry about anything. This is a security company, and even if the cops suspect you're here, they'd have to prove it, and that's going to be hard when I don't have to let them on my property." He gave her a wink and then stood. "I need to touch base with the rest of the crew, but Mina, keep me posted on anything you need my help with."

"You got it, boss."

"Charlie, out," he said, leaving the room.

"I'll take my leave as well," Iris said. "I've got some other cases to get back to, but once those are caught up, I'll dig into Miles and his friend."

"Iris, wait," Mina said, standing, too. "The Miles angle is urgent. Let's figure out who can take your other cases while you focus on this."

She turned to Reece. "Take Skylar back to the cabin and let her rest while she listens to the videos. You can keep searching, too."

Reece nodded, knowing without her saying it whom he should keep searching for—Silas Sullivan.

Chapter Fifteen

It had been a long day, but it wasn't over yet. Thankfully, the recliner in the cabin was a comfortable place to sit and watch the videos from Binate while Reece worked on whatever Reece worked on. She had finally convinced him that it was wiser for her to watch the videos while he worked on finding more information on Miles to help Iris. He didn't know Miles, so he wouldn't catch something on the videos that would give him away. Only she could do that. If it was there to find, she would.

However, her focus was split, making it hard to concentrate on the videos. What had happened today at Secure One weighed on her— both the health and personal implications. Autonomic dysreflexia was a dangerous condition that could turn deadly. Her level of spinal cord injury made it more common, but the episodes she'd had so far were few and far between. It probably wasn't fair to compare anything she was going through right now to her day-to-day life. This was anything but that, the least of which was being in a tight space with Reece Palmer for days on end. While she thought about him every day, it was easier to pretend she didn't care about him when he wasn't protecting her—when he wasn't sleeping next to her in a buttery-soft, king-size bed.

Her body was...not attractive, to say the least. After years in a wheelchair, gravity had taken its toll, and while she was able to work out her upper body to a degree, there was nothing she could do for her paralyzed abdominal muscles. She didn't want to think about her legs. They used to be what she was most proud of. She'd had lean, strong, long legs that did everything she asked of them on the field without hesitation. They were still long, but they were also thin, weak and shriveled. The skin and bones reminded her every day of her choices, the good and the bad.

Reece walked into the room with two plates in his hands. "Sadie brought dinner. Selina suggested you stay put for the night, so she made us some to-go plates."

"That was so kind of her," Skylar said, setting the laptop aside so she could take the plate he held out. "Everyone here truly goes above and beyond."

Reece sat on the couch beside her chair and handed her silverware and a napkin. "It's that military mentality of leaving no man behind. They carried it over into their civilian work, and it's served them well so far. What Cal has built in this little town since he first moved here is nothing short of brilliant. He started as a mercenary and ended up running one of the most sought-after security companies in the nation."

"What's funny is that he doesn't act like he knows that."

"He knows, but he also knows that we got to where we are as a team. You'll never see him resting on his laurels. He's not wired that way."

"I can tell," she said with a chuckle. "Cal didn't have to be in that meeting today, but he wanted to keep his thumb on the pulse of what was developing, even if he left it in Mina's capable hands."

"You picked up on that, did you?" he asked with a wink.

"Does Sadie do freelance chef work? I could get behind homemade Swedish meatballs like these on a regular basis."

"I wish!" His laughter was easy for the first time all day. "It's always sad when I'm here for a week and then go home to my TV dinners and takeout."

"You've been single a long time and still don't cook?"

"I do, sometimes," he said with a shrug. "Honestly, it's more depressing to cook for one than to heat something up and eat it in front of the computer. It makes you feel less alone."

"I hear that," she agreed, not making eye contact. "Your computer is my easel, but it's the same concept. Since Mom and Dad moved to Florida, it's been difficult. I have friends and people I hang out with, but there are a lot of empty hours to fill."

"You didn't want to move to Florida?"

Dropping her fork, she set the plate aside on the end table. Sadie's meatballs were filling, and she didn't want to get sick after the day she'd had. "We talked about it, but it would have meant finding an accessible place there to accommodate my needs, which wasn't impossible, but it would have limited my parents when this was their time to make a new life. They had gone through enough and deserved the freedom to enjoy the life they'd worked hard for all those years. I didn't want to hold them back by wheeling around after them."

"I know your parents don't feel that way about it, Sky."

It was easier to stare at the opposite wall than to make eye contact with him when she talked about her family. "We went through a lot with my brother, Land. Stuff that you don't even know about. There were things I never told you because I knew you'd kill him if you knew."

He tipped his head to the side. "You're not wrong. Especially if it involved him touching you."

"That time you caught him? It wasn't the first," she admitted, shame filling her voice. She glanced at him and noticed the light go out in that gray eye while fire filled the blue one. They always said people with two different-colored eyes could see heaven and earth simultaneously. She was starting to wonder if that was true.

"So help me God, if I find that man alive, he won't be for long," Reece ground out, his plate clattering on the table as he tossed it aside to take her hand. "Why didn't you tell me? And don't say it's because I'd hurt Silas. You weren't bothered in the least when I beat him senseless in the seventh grade."

"I was ashamed, okay?" she asked, defense clear in her tone as she tried to pull away.

He held tight to her hand and breathed deeply through his nose. "How long, Sky?"

"A couple of years," she whispered, staring at their joined hands. "It wasn't all the time, and sometimes I wondered if I dreamed it."

"Sounds like something a victim would say." She could tell he was trying to be gentle but wanted to pound on something. Probably her brother's face. Reece wasn't a violent man except when it came to Silas. It was like he could see under her brother's skin to the monster he was when no one else could.

"I'm still mad they didn't kick him out the moment he turned eighteen," Reece said, holding her hand and leaning in as though he couldn't stand the distance between them. She knew that wasn't true. Not after what happened today, but having someone to talk to who cared about her felt nice. "I suppose by then it was clear that something was very wrong with Silas."

"My parents knew something was wrong, but Silas refused to go to therapy. After you beat him and I told them why, they insisted on getting him help. We were all scared out of our minds, and the worst part was I couldn't talk to anyone about it. After many years of therapy, I know it wasn't my fault. My parents did their best with the hand they'd been dealt. When my accident happened, everything fell apart with Silas."

"Why did your parents work so hard to find him after he left? If everything you said is true, weren't they happy he was out of their lives?

He was twenty-three by then and could more than go it on his own."

"You're forgetting that he was their child. We don't have children, so it's easy for us to judge what they did or didn't do."

"Fair," Reece agreed. "I'm not judging them. I'm trying to understand their thinking."

He was more likely digging for an angle to help him find Silas, but she wouldn't bring that up. He could look all he wanted. Silas was dead.

"I asked my dad about it after the third private investigator couldn't find him. If I'm honest, his explanation gutted me."

"He felt guilty, right?"

Skylar made the so-so hand. "Guilty in the respect that he worried letting Silas out in the world unmanaged meant—"

"He might hurt someone."

She nodded for a long time before she spoke. "Silas had real issues, and leaving home wouldn't fix them. Staying on his meds and going to therapy would help him, but it's doubtful that happened."

"You always use past tense with Silas. Why?"

"Because whether he's alive or not, he's dead to me, Reece. We were never siblings. We were two people who lived in the same house. By the time I was born, he was way too old for us to bond with any meaningful kind of relationship."

"The age difference was there, but that can work in a family's favor sometimes," Reece pointed out.

"Sure, if everyone is mentally stable, but we both know Silas was never that. Now we know why. It was no one's fault, but we had to protect ourselves. The therapist finally convinced my parents that they weren't responsible for the choices Silas made once he left their house."

"But you think he's dead and buried?"

"Definitely dead. Don't know about buried. It's been thirteen years since he left, and we haven't heard anything from him. The fact that you're wasting time looking for him is like watching someone spin their wheels in the mud. Walk away, Reece. Not only is Silas not behind whatever is going on, but we're wasting time and energy that could be better used."

"Sweetheart, it's my job to cover every angle of a case. Pretending Silas is dead works for you, and that's okay, given the history you share, but it doesn't work in a case like this. We have to look under every rock for anyone who wants to do you harm."

"He's dead, Land. And even if he isn't, he—"

"Isn't capable of carrying out a plot like this. I know," he said, holding up his hand to her. "I want you to know I agree with you, but I have to do my job. The last thing I want to do is bring him back into your life, but we have to know if he has anything to do with this. Right?"

This time, she held his gaze, and what she saw in those eyes of heaven and earth said he meant every word. His search for Silas wasn't to hurt her. It was to help her. "You're right," she admitted. "As much as I want to pretend that he's dead and buried, until we have proof of that, it would be foolish not to consider his involvement."

"Did you come up with anything on the videos to help us yet?" he asked, motioning at the laptop.

"No, but I'm not giving up. I will watch them ten times if I have to. Reading the comments on the petition page propped me up. There wasn't one comment that agreed with whoever this is about me being responsible for these gallery crimes."

Reece squeezed her hand and smiled. "Hang on to that. Remember that when you return to your normal life, you won't be shunned in the art world. No one believes you're responsible for this."

"It might be better if they did," she said slowly, her brow going up.

"I don't follow," he said, leaning back on the couch.

"Hear me out," she said, turning on her side a bit to see him better. "If Binate thinks people are buying his story, it might benefit us. If suddenly he sees the tide turning against me, he might ride that wave."

"Embolden this Binate guy to do or say something that tips us off to his real identity?" Reece asked, following her train of thought.

"That's what I'm starting to wonder, Land. Should we be feeding his ego rather than fighting it? Can we do that without him knowing it's a setup?"

"Fake comments on a Facebook page? Mina could do that in her sleep. It would have to be gradual, though, so he doesn't suspect it's a ruse. You might be on to something here, angel. Let's call Mina and get her opinion. If there's a way, she will know it."

Angel.

That new nickname was far more dangerous to her heart than *Sky* would ever be. Sky was a throwback to their childhood. It was easy and filled her with the warmth of yesteryear. *Angel* filled her with a different kind of warmth— the kind of warmth that she'd experienced this morning when his lips were on hers. It was also the kind of warmth that would break her heart night after night the moment she was alone again.

She couldn't help but wonder why now. Why tonight? After what he had witnessed this morning, he should have been walking away. Then again, maybe it had everything to do with what had happened this morning. He wasn't using it as a term of endearment as much as a way to coddle her now that he saw the truth about her fragility.

Her mind wandered back to the look in his eyes this morning when he held her face in his hands and kept her calm as Selina saved her life. That didn't feel like coddling. That felt like love.

Chapter Sixteen

The cursor sat blinking, a reminder that he hadn't found his man. How did a person live in the world for thirteen years without any identification? He glanced at the woman asleep in the recliner and sighed. He couldn't give up. Reece had never wanted to be a hero for anyone until today, when he was so hopelessly useless that he would have traded his life for hers. He couldn't do that physically, but he would work through the night if it meant finding the jerk who was tormenting her.

Frustrated, Reece flicked to the Facebook tab and checked the comments on the petition page. The first planted comment had arrived.

It takes no brainpower to believe Skylar Sullivan could commit these crimes or hire some flunky to do it. Lord knows she makes enough money on that garbage she passes off as art.

A smile lifted his lips. Mina had played to Miles's beliefs perfectly but in a way that didn't feel fake or forced. He left the tab open to hear when Binate replied to the comment—and he had no doubt he would. Mina had gotten behind the idea quickly. She could see they were at a stalemate until they lulled Binate into a sense that someone was on his side. While they couldn't stop the organic comments defending Sky, they could make sure to plant enough negative ones to start stroking the ego of a very fragile man. Maybe they couldn't prove it was Miles, but at this point, Reece didn't find it hard to believe he was involved in some way. His money was still on Silas, though.

Staring at the blinking cursor again, Reece ran down what he'd done so far to find Silas. Had he crossed every t and dotted every i? Was there a database he'd missed or a program he hadn't used? A quick consult with his list said he'd exhausted every avenue to find this guy. His gut burned with the knowledge that Silas had been abusing her for years and she'd told no one. He understood why—that was a common situation victims found themselves in, but it still made him feel as impotent as he'd been this morning when she was dying before his very eyes. The same way he'd felt that night on the field when all he could do was tell her it would be okay even though they both knew it wouldn't be. In just a hair over three days, Skylar Sullivan had consumed him again. When this was over and she was safe, he had zero idea how he would get her out of his system. Not that he'd had much success with that over the last decade, but he'd managed by simply ignoring the pain of having half of his soul torn away every morning when he woke up. He filled his life with endless jobs, conferences and degrees to hide how empty it had become.

Now that he'd had a little taste of being whole again and having tasted her, Reece was well aware he'd never return to that kind of life. When he'd brushed his lips against hers this morning, his soul fractured. An ache engulfed him, leaving him drowning in sorrow at the time they'd spent apart. At the same time, he rode a wave of pleasure and completeness at being connected to her that he had never experienced with anyone in his life. He'd been with women, but no one left him feeling so hopeful and hopeless with a simple kiss the way Sky had.

Then, in a dark moment, he'd taken her in his arms, and it had become clear that there was no way to return to the life he had led a week ago. When he glanced at the screen, it reminded him that a week ago, Sky had also been living a different kind of life, and if he didn't figure out who wanted to destroy her, a week from now, she could be sitting in a jail cell. He set his jaw and refused even to consider that possibility.

Focused again on the case before him, he reviewed everything, only to reach the same conclusion: Silas had fallen off the face of the earth the moment he drove out of Duluth. That was just a mirage, though. He gave Silas far more credit than Skylar did when it came to his level of intelligence, so there was only one explanation—he had to be using an alias. His gut told him that her brother was behind this, which meant he was very much alive and living as someone other than Silas Sullivan. Cracking the code on the alias was the problem.

Extended family. Always start with extended family.

He remembered the lesson from one of his first professors in college. Spine straight, he put his hands on the keyboard. The Nebraska grandparents were Skylar's mom's parents. What was her maiden name? He could ask Sky, but he didn't want to wake her if he didn't have to. She was exhausted after their day, and her body needed to recover. Also, after her soliloquy about the futility of looking for Silas, he didn't want to bring it up again until he had proof that her brother was alive and well. He was out there somewhere dressed as Anonymous and spewing hatred for a woman who didn't deserve any of this. Reece might not have been able to catch and protect her that night fourteen years ago, but he would do it this time if it killed him.

Pear Pickin' Farms, where the sweetness lasts year-round.

Tobias and Marlene Pear, he typed into the computer, remembering the long-ago tagline from their orchard. He'd never been there, but he and Sky would tease each other with that line for years. Funny the things you forgot until it was a matter of life and death.

The screen filled with information about the deaths of Tobias and Marlene ten years ago. They'd passed away together due to carbon monoxide poisoning. His gaze flew to Sky, who was still slumbering in the chair. He'd had no idea they'd passed, but such a tragic, preventable way made it that much harder. He couldn't help but wonder if her Grandma Barbara was alive, so he quickly googled her name, only to discover there were way too many Barbara Sullivans to weed through. His attention was back on Silas, and he opened one of his background programs. He typed in, Silas Pear, age thirty-seven United States. He hit Return and let it spin, not surprised when no one showed up. That would have been too easy. What was Silas's middle name? Joseph, which was his dad's name. No, he wouldn't make it that obvious. If he was trying to become someone else, he'd have to be far more subtle, or the detectives the family had hired would have found him. He removed the age, and again, nothing came up. Reece tried several combinations using his first initial, his grandfather's name and any other combination of his middle name but came up empty.

Maybe he wasn't using Pear as a last name, which made this a game of finding the needle in the haystack. A glance at the clock told him it was after midnight and he should get some sleep and tackle this again in the morning, but his mind was far too activated to sleep. Since Sky was comfortable, he'd keep working. His mind was tumbling with all the information he knew about Silas. He was older than them by enough years that he'd been a teenager when they were still in grade school. Their experiences were vastly different, but Reece forced his mind to calm and methodically think through the conversations he'd had with Silas. Once Silas became a teen, Reece and Sky had tried to avoid him as much as possible—especially after he beat the stuffing out of him.

Reece stood on the patio with a cold can of pop in his hand and watched Sky doing handstands and backflips in the yard while Silas yammered on about his video games. Whoopee, so some character in a video game had the same last name as him. What good did that do if you couldn't even play the game as that character? He didn't understand the fascination with video games. Sure, they're fun when it's raining or you're bored, but revolving your life around them was a bit much.

With a jolt, he opened a tab and googled video game characters with the last name Sullivan. Before he could take a breath, he had an entire page of results. The first one? Sergeant Tom Sullivan from *Call of Duty*. That was Silas's favorite game.

"Got you," he whispered as he returned to his program and typed in the name. There would be a lot of hits, but he could whittle them down quickly. Once it was down to the two dozen within the age range, he added an S as a middle initial just for grins. Bingo. That brought it down to six. *Why not go all the way?* He thought as he typed in Silas as the middle name. The boy he used to know had always thought he was the most cunning of video game players, and he wouldn't be able to resist mixing his name with the hero of his favorite fake war game.

Fingers crossed, he hit Enter and waited not so patiently while the program did its work.

Then, before his very eyes, a thirty-five-year-old version of Silas Sullivan filled the screen. Without taking his eyes off the picture, he reached for his phone.

Chapter Seventeen

"Angel, I need you to wake up," Reece whispered in her ear.

Blinking, she glanced up into his face. Unable to resist, she smoothed her hand over his soft beard, and he smiled.

"I need to shave. It's been a busy few days."

"I like it," she said with a smile. "I still see you as the boy I used to know. This shows me the man you've become."

His blue eye darkened to navy as he gazed at her, drinking her in as though she wasn't a shell of a woman in a shriveled body. "I see you as the stunning woman you've become from that girl I used to know. You've left me breathless for days."

The eye roll happened, even though she knew it was rude. "Sorry, but, Reece, have you looked at me? I'm a hot mess, both physically and apparently in life. 'Stunning woman,'" she said, using air quotes, "is not this." She motioned down her body as he shook his head slowly.

"I understand why you feel that way, but it doesn't mean I do, Sky. We need to put that aside for now and get you to bed. Selina said the catheter should drain freely tonight to prevent issues."

"What time is it?" she asked, rubbing her eyes. "The last thing I remember was watching Facebook videos."

He chuckled and gave her a wink as he lifted the blanket off her and folded it. "It's nearly 2:00 a.m. You fell asleep, so I covered you and let you get some rest while I worked. Now, it's time for both of us to be in bed. I'll carry you to the bedroom and return for your chair."

"Not necessary," she said immediately. "I only need help putting the recliner down." If there was one thing she hated about her disability, it was recliners. If they weren't powered, she couldn't push the footrest down to get out of the chair and always required help.

"It is necessary," he said, bending down and sliding his hands under her back and knees. "It's necessary for me to feel you in my arms again as a reminder that I didn't lose you this morning. Give me that, please?"

Never able to deny him anything when he asked with a pure and open heart, she nodded and allowed herself to be lifted and carried to the bedroom, where he lowered her to bed, which had already been prepared for the night. Once she rested comfortably on the pillows, she pointed to the bathroom without making eye contact. Shame filled her, but his need to carry her to the bed meant she had to open herself to embarrassment again.

"Would you get my drain bag? It's hanging in the bathroom."

"Nope, got it right here," he said, lifting the tubing for her to see before he lifted her shirt far enough to reveal the catheter taped to her abdomen. Selina had suggested she leave it taped at an angle rather than coil it to prevent it from kinking.

"What are you doing?" she asked, grabbing his hand to stop him. "I can do it. Please, get my chair."

"I'm connecting your catheter to the bag. Selina showed me how."

"I can do it, Land. Please," she begged.

He held up his hands and then motioned for her to do it. It was then that she realized she couldn't see the connections while lying flat.

Frustrated, she flopped her head back onto the pillow and sighed. "I can't see the connection. If you'll get my chair, I can transfer to that and do it."

"Or, I can connect it in five seconds to save you the effort required to transfer twice."

Finally, she nodded and let him carry out the process until it was connected, and she heard the catheter draining into the bag.

Reece lowered her shirt and covered her with the blanket before kneeling beside the bed. "It's okay to accept help sometimes, angel. It doesn't mean you're weak. It means someone cares about you enough to take that burden off your shoulders for a few moments."

With her eyes squeezed shut, she nodded, but mostly, she wanted him to leave long enough for her to fight back the tears. She knew she'd lost the battle when his finger trailed down her cheek to wipe one away. "Could you have picked something less gross to help me with?"

"Angel, there's nothing gross about what I just did. My God, I'd do it fifty times a day if it meant you never had to go through what you went through this morning. It's a basic human function that we all do. You do it differently. That doesn't mean it's gross or shameful. I think it's an amazing advancement for spinal cord injury patients. You don't have to do the intermittent catheterization that used to rule your life and make you sick. I know I don't live in your body or understand what it's like to do that, but I do want to learn how to help you."

"Why?" she asked, her voice barely above a whisper. The light was low in the room, and the darkness and shadows made her feel braver than she was as she wiped a tear from her face. "Why do you even care?"

"I've always cared about you, Sky, and I always will. We can't go back to pretending that the other person doesn't exist once this is over. At least I can't, so if I learn how to help you, at least I can be there for you as a friend, right?"

"I don't want to lose you as a friend again," she agreed with a whisper. It was her way of telling him that all they could be was friends, and the look in his eye told her he understood that.

"Then you won't," he promised, kissing her forehead. "I'm going to get your chair. Be right back."

Land stood and strode from the room, so she quickly wiped her face with the soft sheet. He wouldn't be gone long, and she wanted to get herself together before he returned. He wanted to help, and she'd allow it for now. It felt good to feel cared for, but once this was over, that was a different story. He had his own life, and staying in touch, while it sounded nice, would be far too painful to her heart when she couldn't have him in her life for all time.

Once he had the chair next to the bed for her, he climbed onto his side, keeping a sheet between them, and then covered himself with a spare blanket. He propped himself on his arm and slid the other across her chest to cup her shoulder.

"We need to talk."

"Can it wait until morning? We're both exhausted." The last thing she wanted to do was talk about their relationship, or lack thereof, at 2:00 a.m.

"I'm afraid not. I found Silas."

"What?" she asked, turning to meet his gaze. "How? Why? Where?" Her moan that followed the rapid questions said exactly how she felt about knowing he'd dug up part of her past. "I wanted him to stay buried."

"He is," Land said, raising his hand to stroke her cheek with his thumb. "He was using the alias Tom Sullivan."

"Oh, God, from that video game!" she exclaimed. "He was obsessed with that game. Why didn't I think of that all those years ago?"

"It probably didn't cross your mind that he'd use an alias. I'm surprised the private detectives never asked your parents."

"They may have, but I was pretty out of it for those first few years after he left. So, he's dead?"

"Yes," Land said with a sigh. "Once I found his alias, I could trace him to a death certificate in Colorado."

"Colorado? That's an odd state for him to pick."

Land opened his mouth as though he was about to say something, but paused. "There are a lot of places to hide in Colorado."

"When did he die? Did you find out anything else about him? What did he do for work?"

"According to the death certificate, he died three years ago. The cause of death was drowning. There wasn't a lot of information I could find about him regarding his life or work history. Iris will dig into it in the morning. I'm sorry, Sky. I hated to be the one to tell you this, but you had to know."

"I'm not upset, Land. I'm relieved, actually. It's like that weird ball of nerves that he might show up in our lives is gone. I always assumed he was dead, but with no proof, there was always a lingering worry. That's gone now. I can't thank you enough for that."

He kept stroking her cheek with his thumb, all his attention focused on her. "He was still your brother. It's okay to grieve the innocence that was lost."

"Trust me, that happened a long time ago. Seriously, I'm solidly relieved, Land. The only hard part will be telling my parents, but that can wait until this is all figured out and I can see them in person. Please, make sure no one from Secure Watch tells them."

"It has already been said," he assured her with a smile. "I'm proud of you."

"Why? Because I'm so inspirational?" Her eye roll was hard and practiced but also defensive. If she could keep him focused on her anger with life, he'd learn he didn't want any part of hers.

"I see through your defenses, angel. Your walls aren't hard for me to scale when I know you as well as I do, even fourteen years later. I'm proud of you for the way you're plowing through this situation. Losing your identity is difficult, but you're hanging in there and working through it with us. Not everyone can do that. I've dealt with people who curl up in a ball and shut out the world. We can solve this if you can hang in a bit longer."

"I want to be part of the solution. My life already involves enough situations where people have to do things for me. I can help with this and want to do that, so you don't have to treat me with kid gloves."

His laughter was soft when it filled the room. "Oh, that is the last thing I would ever do. There's never been a situation you haven't tackled head-on. We can do this together as long as we're honest with each other."

Land leaned down and planted a kiss on her forehead, his lips soft and warm as they hesitated there for a moment, as though he was thinking about doing so much more. Instead, he pulled back and shut off the small lamp on the bedside table, plunging the room into darkness. This was one time she was grateful for darkness. It gave her time to stuff all those feelings she had for this man back into the box where she kept them so she could live without crying every single day he was missing from her life.

Then he rolled over and cupped her shoulder, his face just inches from hers as he snuggled into his pillow. It felt like they were an old married couple who had slept this way for years. The tears leaked from her eyes, because he remembered how she liked to be touched. She could feel her shoulders and had told him early on that when she needed to feel human touch, that was the best place to hold her. He'd done it ever since. God, how she loved the sensation of his protective hand on her as he relaxed into sleep.

Carefully, she swiped at the tears while trying not to disturb him in his sleep. Those tears represented loss. Losing her future after the accident, losing Land and now, losing another piece of her family. However, she wasn't upset by Silas's loss. She was upset about losing the chance to face him again and tell him how he'd hurt her. Her therapist had told her that if she ever got that chance, she should take it. She needed to put all the negativity back on his shoulders to be free of them. That was no longer possible. She thought about the letter she'd written. Had they ever found him, she'd planned to mail it to him, but now, even that option was gone. When this was over, she'd fold it into a paper boat and set it free on Lake Superior, where it could disintegrate and sink to the depths, never to be seen again, just like Silas.

With a deep breath in, she knew that was the right decision. Then he feathered his thumb across her cheek to wipe a tear, shattering her heart into a million little pieces with that slight touch. Making the right decision about Land would be the hardest decision of her life.

Chapter Eighteen

Cal walked into the meeting with his jaw ticking. Immediately, Reece knew whatever he had to say wouldn't be good.

"Sorry to interrupt," Cal said to Mina, who motioned at him to take the floor. "There's been a development." He glanced down at the paper in his hand. "Around 2:00 a.m., a body was found on the Lakewalk in Duluth. When the police arrived, they identified the victim as Miles Bradshaw, age thirty-five."

Sky's gasp was loud in the quiet room. "No. No. That's not true—no. It can't be."

Sliding his arm around Sky's shoulders, Reece scooted closer to her chair, hating that the wheel got in the way of them connecting hip to hip. "My assumption is the cause of death wasn't natural."

"Not unless you call blunt-force trauma natural."

"Nope," Reece answered, popping the *P*. "No one saw anything?"

"Whoever left him there did so while avoiding all the cameras."

"Wait, left him there?" Reece asked with a brow raised.

"That was also my second question. My police contact says there wasn't enough blood or splatter when compared to his injuries for it to have happened there."

"What is going on?" Sky asked, mournful and angry. "Do you think this is connected to my case?" She was starting to recover from the shock, so he rubbed her back a bit before releasing her.

"It could be a coincidence," Cal said slowly.

"And you know what I say about coincidences," Mina said with a snort.

"Coincidences are easily manufactured," Iris, Cal and Reece said in unison, playing to Mina's mantra.

"She's right, though," Iris said. "There is no way his death isn't related to this whole mess."

"But there's no way Camille is capable of killing him," Sky insisted. "She's smaller than me, and Miles was a big guy."

"There is always a way," Cal said with a brow raised. "And one of those ways is to hire someone to do it for you. Not always the smartest regarding the trust factor, but it happens more than anyone thinks."

"What are the police saying? They can't possibly think Skylar had anything to do with this?" Reece asked.

"Even though there was a note in his wallet that said this?" Cal handed him the paper, and he read it while trying to keep it from Sky.

"'If I'm dead, Skylar Sullivan did it.'" Sky's eyes rolled so hard that Reece feared they'd never return to center. "Lord, he was so dramatic," she said between clenched teeth. "Tell me the cops don't believe that?"

"They have to investigate it, of course, but as of right now, they have no leads. Not only are you incapable of that kind of killing physically, but you couldn't transport him anywhere. Then we're back to the idea of hiring someone, which would be difficult for you right now, considering you're on the run from your other warrant."

"That's what the police think? That I'm 'on the run'?" she asked, using air quotes.

Cal shrugged in a way that told Reece he was holding back a smile. "Well, no. The police think you're hiding out at Secure One while we try to figure out who's setting you up. They're okay with pretending you're on the run for a bit longer since they can't find proof you have been in any of the cities with vandalized galleries or took out large sums of cash to pay someone else to do it."

"That's because I didn't," Sky said, her words tight. "Could they link Miles to any of them?"

"I don't believe they were trying," Cal answered.

"But we have been, and the answer is yes to several," Iris said. "That's what I wanted to bring to your attention today."

Skylar glanced between all of them. "Do you think with Miles's death the vandalism will stop?"

Cal lowered himself to a chair and leaned forward, clasping his hands together, his metal and plastic fingers clicking into place around his flesh and bones. Cal had lost half of his fingers on his right hand while in the service, but the prosthesis he wore was so perfectly fitted to him that he could use the prosthetic finger to pull a trigger with deadly aim.

"I'm going to be real with you here, Sky. Someone killed Miles, which means—"

"Someone else is pulling the strings." Reece felt her heavy sigh all the way to his bones. "I should have thought of that. Even if Miles was doing the vandalism, that doesn't mean the person behind his death won't keep doing it."

"Hey," Reece said, rubbing her neck again to calm her. "You've had a lot thrown at you in the last few hours."

"And you don't do this for a living," Mina added. "That's why you've got us."

"We've got you," Iris assured her, still not making eye contact. "We may not know who is behind this yet, but we won't give up until we do."

"What she said," Cal said with a wink. "We aren't giving up. I was sorry to hear about your brother. I'm sure that wasn't the kind of news you expected to hear during this time."

"Thank you for your concern, but it's a relief to know he's dead and not out there hurting or abusing anyone else. My brother had problems, and he took a lot of them out on me. There was no love lost between us, and truthfully, I'm glad he's dead and buried. That's a part of my life I am happy to put behind me."

You could hear a pin drop in the room, and Reece kept his hand on her neck to let her know he supported her.

"I'm sorry, that was dirty laundry I didn't need to air."

"No need to apologize to us," Mina said with a shake of her head.

Cal turned to Mina. "Have there been any videos uploaded to the Facebook page today?"

"I haven't gotten any notifications," Reece said, pointing at his tablet. "I have it set up to alert me."

Mina held up her finger and clicked around on her screen. After a few moments of silence, she let out an oof and leaned back in her chair. "There were no videos, but look."

She clicked, and the screen on the wall mirroring hers lit up. It showed that the page's owner had responded to every negative comment. "Those responses started about five thirty this morning and went until nine thirty."

"Which means Miles wasn't running that page," Reece said.

"It doesn't appear so," Mina agreed.

"The IP address for the first few comments came up as overseas," Iris said. "I'll check these new comments to see if that's changed, but I'm sure they're using a VPN." Anyone capable of taking control of Sky's digital signature would certainly use a virtual private network to avoid detection.

"I agree." Reece glanced at everyone in the room. "I feel like whoever is behind this just sent us a checkmate message with Miles."

"From one security guy to the other, same," Cal said.

"Maybe Camille *is* behind this," Skylar insisted. "Miles was a puppy when it came to her. What's to say she didn't have other guys doing her bidding, too?"

"Trust me," Cal said, leaning back in his

chair, "that's the working theory now. Someone is behind this, so all we can do is wait for another message or finally crack through the Facebook page to see who's behind it."

"I'm just afraid by the time we wait for another message to arrive, another gallery will be damaged, or someone else will be hurt," Skylar whispered, her gaze taking in all the comments on the board.

Reece was sure everyone else felt the same way, so when no one said anything, she snapped off the brakes on her chair and wheeled out of the room.

THE SUN WAS setting over the manufactured pond at the back of the property. Skylar couldn't get over how gorgeous the land was, and she truly appreciated the little bit of peace and quiet she got sitting there watching the sun sink below the horizon. Besides an arduous trek back to the cabin across the grass, she was safe. Since the meeting this morning, she'd tried to stay away from the case, but as night neared, she would have to face Reece again. He'd given her an update when she woke up from a nap earlier but hadn't pressured her to take part in the investigation or to try to focus her thoughts on the videos. Even if the person behind the mask was Miles, he was dead now. Dead because they were connected. They were missing something, but she couldn't figure it out. Then again, it was more like missing someone—a key player in the campaign to destroy Skylar Sullivan. The only person left whom she dealt with regularly with any hostility toward her wasn't capable of killing a grown man. Was she capable of hiring someone to do it? Well, Skylar couldn't deny the answer to that question was yes. Camille was gregarious and gorgeous. She could easily convince someone to do her bidding, and she sold high-priced art pieces, so she could afford to pay for it.

"I've been looking for you," Land said as he approached her from the direction of the cottage.

"Sorry, I wanted to sketch the sun as it set over the pond," she explained, motioning at her sketch pad.

"I don't blame you," he said, his hand to his head as he stared at the sinking orb. "I always make it a point to watch the sun rise or set at least once when I'm here. It's different than in the city."

"When this is all over, I want to make this into a stained-glass piece for the cafeteria," she explained. "It's not much, but it will come from my heart for what they've done for me."

Land squeezed her shoulder with a smile as

he gazed down at her. "They'd be lucky to have an original Skylar Sullivan piece."

"Not if we don't find the person behind this," she sighed as she closed the book. "I'm sorry I checked out earlier. My brain couldn't take any more."

"Everyone understood," he promised, smoothing a hand down her cheek. "You hadn't even had time to deal with Silas's death when we dropped Miles on you. Did you get any rest?"

"Some," she answered, glancing up at him. "I haven't slept well the last few nights, so I needed it. I also wanted to let the catheter drain freely for a few hours. I always feel like we're a minute away from having to take off again."

"I'm sure you do, but we're safe here until we or the police sort out who's behind these threats against you."

"You mean against the galleries."

After kneeling next to her chair, he tipped his head to the side. "No, I mean against you. They have a vendetta against you. They're just using the galleries to escalate it."

"To what end, though?" she asked in frustration.

"I wish I could say," he whispered, gazing over the water. "I do feel like they'll reveal it soon enough. Killing Miles was a pretty strong escalation."

"What aren't you telling me, Land?" She turned in her chair and tipped his chin to face her. "Did something else happen today?"

"No," he promised while holding her gaze. She could tell by how his pupils didn't react that he was telling the truth. "I'm frustrated with all the dead ends we keep hitting when it comes to Camille Castillo. She's nearly as hard to investigate as Silas was. Sure, we have her name and know where she last lived, but it's like she's fallen off the face of the earth, too."

"Do you think Camille was an alias?"

"We're starting to think so, and now she's using a different one, or she's gone back to using her real name, neither of which we have."

"After dinner, I'll watch the Facebook videos again from the angle of Camille behind the mask. I'll think about my interactions with her while watching them, and maybe I'll pick up on something?"

Despite his skeptical expression, he nodded. "It can't hurt. We've hit a stalemate with this until we get another video or they post something on the petition page."

"Am I wrong, or does it feel like the person behind this has been bolder about posting on the petition page?"

"It's not just you. Mina and Iris also agree. We're hoping that works to our benefit. Since it's a public page, if they want to send you a message, they could use that page to do it."

"Do you still believe they don't know we can see the page where they post the videos?"

"That's a bit murkier, and even Mina agrees with that. Facebook tells a person how many times their video has been watched. Technically, since we're using a dupe page, every time we watch the video, the count shouldn't change, but we can't be sure. Secretly, I hope they know we can see the page. If they know someone else is watching the videos, it might embolden them."

"I hope so, because my nerves can't take too many more days of this."

Land stood and put his hands on his hips. "Sadie sent dinner to the cabin. How about we share it and a movie? Take a little time to relax and think about something else?"

"I'd like that," she agreed with a smile. "It'll let me clear my head and get it back in the game."

While he helped push her back to the cabin, she wondered if she'd ever get back into the art game. If they didn't stop this soon, she would lose everything—including Reece Palmer.

DINNER HAD BEEN DELICIOUS, as always. Sadie's meals were the reason Reece found a way to hang out at Secure One at least once a month. She could cook and had honed her skills since marrying Eric and working full-time as a chef for Cal. She usually cared for Mina and Roman's daughter, Hannah Grace, when she wasn't cooking. He suspected the Secure One family might be growing, though. Earlier, while looking for a cup of coffee, he'd walked down to the cafeteria to find Sadie in the kitchen looking a bit green around the gills as she fried ground beef. He couldn't help but wonder if Sadie and Eric would have an announcement of their own to share soon.

He glanced at Sky, sitting next to him on the couch as they watched the latest mystery flick. She was as invested in it as he was, which was not at all. They'd shared a wonderful dinner, laughing and kidding the way they used to as kids. It was hard to remember their years apart now that they were together again. It was as though nothing had changed, since they could still finish each other's sentences.

"Why did you refuse to date me after we graduated?" he blurted out, groaning at the rough delivery. He'd been thinking about asking it for days and couldn't hold back a second longer.

"What?" she asked, clearly pretending she

didn't understand the question when she most certainly did.

"Right after we graduated, I asked if you'd go on a date with me. You said no. You told me we could be friends but nothing more. Why?"

"You mean other than being paralyzed?" She pushed off his shoulder and sat up straight, grabbing the arm of the couch to steady herself.

"What did being paralyzed have to do with it? It was months after the accident when I asked. You were back to school and just doing outpatient therapy."

"Using a wheelchair every day for the rest of my life had everything to do with it," she said between clenched teeth. "In a split second on that October night, we became different people, Land. You remained you, but I became someone new. Someone even I didn't know yet. There was no way I would subject you to the kind of life I would lead. It was nonstop doctor and therapy appointments, expensive medical equipment, and procedure after procedure. That was not the kind of life I wanted for you."

"Wait, what are you saying?"

"I'm saying that I refused to date you to give you a better life. I didn't want to saddle you with my unexpected circumstances. You walked away from that accident and had a chance to do great things. There was no way I was going to drag you down with me. I wanted you to go out and live your dreams. I wanted you to find a woman who could do everything you loved to do and give you everything I couldn't."

"You're saying that you decided for me what I wanted out of life? What gave you that right?"

"This," she said, transferring into her chair and smacking the tires. "This gave me the right. You should thank me for it!"

"Thank you? I should thank you for deciding my future on my behalf without consulting me? How is that fair?" His questions got louder with each one until he sat on the edge of the couch, vibrating with anger.

"Fair? You want to talk to me about fair? You got a broken wrist. I got this!" She smacked the tires again. "Yes, I decided to go out there that night, and I accept that, but there's nothing fair about this!" Before he could react, she snapped the brakes off and wheeled around him.

"Where are you going?" he asked as she wheeled down the hallway.

"To bed! You're not welcome to join me. Enjoy the couch!"

The door slammed shut, and he growled, slapping a cushion in anger and frustration. Dammit, why did he have to go and open his big mouth? Flicking off the television, he stormed outside to pace on the small porch that held an old-fashioned rocking chair and a small table made from a tree stump.

"Everything okay over there?" Roman had walked out onto his cabin's porch and down the stairs.

"Fine," he growled, running his fingers through his hair.

"It didn't sound like it to me. I couldn't hear what was said, but the tone was loud and clear."

Reece rolled his eyes. "I figured Cal would have better insulation in these things."

"Well, when the windows are open, sound travels."

He'd forgotten about the windows. He'd opened them earlier to cool the house off after the heat of the day. "I totally forgot the windows were open. It's fine. We just had a bit of a disagreement."

Roman leaned against the railing, pulled a beer out of each jacket pocket and handed him one. They popped the tops off and clinked the necks together before taking a drink. The malty liquid turned his stomach when he swallowed, but it wasn't the beer as much as it was having upset the woman in the bedroom.

"Want to talk about it?"

"Not really," Reece said, lowering himself to the rocking chair and taking another swig of the beer.

"Will what just happened somehow interfere with resolving this situation she's in?"

"Probably," he agreed, hanging his head to stare at the porch floor rather than at his friend.

"Did you make an unwelcome advance?"

"Absolutely not!" he growled as he rose to a standing position. "That's not who I am."

Roman tipped his beer at him. "Agreed, so what else would make her angry enough to lock herself in the bedroom?"

With a shoulder-sagging sigh, Reece sat again. "I finally found the courage to ask her why she refused to date me after graduation. She told me she decided I deserved to go out and live my life and not be saddled with someone in her situation."

Roman lifted his brow before he took another sip of his beer. "Yeah, that tracks."

"Excuse me?" Reece stood again, but this time, it was to pace.

"I remember the days right after Mina's amputation. She decided that I was better off without her. I could do so much better than her and deserved someone who could keep up with me physically."

"Those are the same words Sky used on me," Reece admitted, pausing his steps.

"If you give women time to think in that situation, that will always be the answer they arrive at." He shrugged as he took a drink from the bottle. "Hell, we might feel the same if the roles were reversed. Maybe not wanting to be a burden on someone is a human trait, not a gender trait."

With a soft chuckle, Reece shook his head. "The way you say *maybe* tells me it's not a maybe at all."

Roman shrugged again, but this time, it was a confirmation shrug. "You can't blame her for having a different view of life while sitting in a chair you weren't sitting in. She was young, injured, scared and probably embarrassed by what had happened to her body."

No doubt that was the truth. Reece still remembered how she had closed in on herself, refusing to talk to anyone for days while she did nothing but draw. Her parents and doctors told him that drawing was good therapy to help her deal with her injuries and a new way of life, but he hadn't thought so. He'd always thought it gave her too much time to think and not enough time to remember she was still the same person, even if she had to use a chair to get around. It was obvious to him now that he'd been correct.

"I'd venture to say that she's still scared and embarrassed by what has happened to her body. She's pushing you away equally as hard now to fight the attraction she still has for you."

That drew him from his ruminations of the past. "Come again?"

"Dude, if you can't see that girl still has feelings for you, you shouldn't be an investigator. Of course, if you think you're hiding your feelings for her, you're also wrong."

"We're friends, Roman, and barely that. Until four days ago, I hadn't seen her in nearly fourteen years."

"Yet the first person she called when she was in trouble was you."

Before Reece could object, Roman held up his hand and started for the cabin stairs. "I have to check on Hannah and make sure she fell asleep. Before you walk back into that cabin, I suggest you have a game plan for groveling. You're going to need one."

"Gee, thanks," Reece grunted as Roman laughed. He gave Reece a cheeky salute before disappearing inside and shutting the door.

Reece swiped the half-empty beer off the table and finished it in one swallow. Maybe he did need a game plan. Then again, he could always try honesty and see where that got him.

Determined to make things right, he walked inside, closed all the windows and drew a deep breath before knocking on the locked bedroom door.

Chapter Nineteen

There was a knock on the door, and Skylar forced herself not to say anything.

"Sky? Can I come in?"

Biting her tongue, she kept sketching on her pad, hoping he'd go away and leave her alone. She'd heard the front door slam shut and had hoped he would decide to work, but here he was, just fifteen minutes later, bugging her.

"I know you aren't sleeping. I can hear your pencil on the paper."

"How can you hear that?" His soft laughter came from the other side of the door, and she groaned. He'd been baiting her. "Go away, Reece. I'm tired."

"I'm sure you are, but I want to apologize. I'll do it through the door, but it would probably mean more if I didn't have to." She remained silent and, after thirty seconds, heard his sigh through the door. "I'll start by saying I was an insensitive oaf for bringing it up. My timing was never great."

Obviously, he was determined to have his say, so she closed her sketch pad and called out to him. "You can come in. I'm sure the neighbors would appreciate it."

A key slid into the lock before the handle turned, and in walked the man she couldn't stop thinking about—or crying about, for that matter. She swiped at her face with her shoulder just in case there were any stray tears. Not that she could conceal the splotchy red face from the tears she hadn't tried to hide when she was alone. Reece walked to the bed and sat as she fiddled with her pencil to avoid eye contact.

"I'm sorry," he said, swiping a piece of hair off her forehead before he let his finger trail down across her tearstained face. "Hang on."

Surprised, she waited while he ran the water in the bathroom before returning with a warm washcloth that he held to her face. He gently blotted her salty skin before handing it to her. She held it to her cheek, allowing the warmth to soak into her skin and soothe her.

"If I could take back the last thirty minutes, I would," he said, taking her other hand. "You're dealing with enough right now. You don't need to worry about the past."

"I shouldn't have overreacted," she said, staring at their hands linked together.

"And I should have considered your side of the situation before I got angry."

Her shrug was jerky as she tried to push back the tears. "We were both navigating adult situations without the benefit of adult maturity."

"You were in pain, scared, angry and—"

"Jealous." She'd rather say it than hear it from his lips.

"Jealous of me?"

Her nod made her lip tremble. The time had come to admit the truth to the man she had pushed away as a boy.

"You were jealous that I wasn't hurt in the accident that changed your life."

"That's not true!" Her vehement denial set him back a step. "You were hurt, and I don't just mean your arm. It was easy to see that the effects of the accident would always be with you. The jealousy was more about your dreams still being alive while mine were dead and buried. If that accident hadn't happened and you'd asked me to go on a date after graduation, the answer would have been a resounding yes. Instead, right or wrong, I chose—"

"Me," he said with a nod. "You set your wants and needs aside to give me a chance at the kind of life we'd always talked about having, even if you could no longer be part of it."

"And you did, so it was worth it." Her words

were filled with sadness, but the idea that he was happy reminded her that she wanted nothing but good things for him.

Slowly, he lifted her hand to his lips and brushed a kiss across her knuckles. "Maybe I had the professional success we'd always talked about, but personally, I'm still that boy asking his best friend out on a date. After I graduated, I stayed in Duluth, hoping to catch a glimpse of you somewhere. Sometimes, I'd see you sketching on the Lakewalk, and I'd sit in my truck and watch you, thinking about what could have been. I set up Google Alerts for your name so I would get alerts when you were having a show somewhere. I'd go to as many as I could in disguise to see your work and maybe, just maybe, the beautiful blue eyes of the girl I couldn't stop thinking about no matter how many years passed."

"Seriously?"

In answer, he just brushed another kiss across her knuckles.

"I wanted you to go out, meet someone, marry, have babies. You deserve that, Reece."

"So do you, Sky. This," he said, motioning at the wheelchair, "doesn't mean you have to give up on all of your dreams."

"You were my dream, Land. The only dream that ever mattered to me." Before she could finish her thought, his lips were on hers, pressing her head back into the pillows.

With her eyes closed, she let the kiss happen, responding to his touch in a way that left no doubt in her mind that she would love this man forever, even if they would always be star-crossed lovers. When he slid his hand up her ribs to cup her breast, it took her by surprise. She moaned, only to immediately break the kiss and push his hand away.

"Land, stop," she said with a panted breath. "You can't touch me like that."

He moved his hand immediately. "Did I hurt you?"

"No," she said, shaking her head to keep the tears at bay. "You didn't hurt me. Having you touch me like that is all I've ever dreamed about, but it can't happen."

"Why not?" he asked, his forehead balanced on hers as he gazed into her eyes. It was hard to lie to his face, so she didn't.

"Because I'm a weak woman, and if it happens, I won't be able to give you up when this is over. The first time nearly killed me. I can't do it again."

"Who says you have to?"

"This," she said, motioning at the chair and around the room. "There's so much about my life that you don't see, Land."

"Maybe, but you didn't allow me to learn about you, either."

"You want to learn about me?" she asked, tugging on the blanket until he shifted so she could pull it off. "Fine. Let's start with my legs." Rather than meet his gaze, she just waved her hands at her legs. "Remember how strong they once were?" She lifted one with her hands, watching it fall to the bed in a tangle. "Noodles, Reece. They're like noodles." Before he could react, she lifted her shirt and lowered her panties. "Then there's this. Isn't this the sexiest thing you've ever seen? Oh, wait, you've seen the whole catheter debacle already. How could I forget? That means you've seen my beautiful para-belly, too. What's that? Well, it's the sagging and bagging of my paralyzed muscles being dragged down by my internal organs. I have to wear a binder during the day so I don't feel like my insides are falling out. Sexy, right? Should we keep going?"

Reece's hand touched hers, and he leaned over her until she was forced to meet his gaze. "Angel, stop. None of this is about your body."

"What is it about then, Land?" she whisper-asked. "This is my body, and there's no changing it."

"I wouldn't want to, Sky. Don't you see? This body has made you who you are today. You would not be the person you are today if that accident hadn't happened. You can look at that as a positive or a negative for sure, and I see both sides, but when I look at you, all I see is strength and determination. I can't sit here and listen to the girl I've cared about my entire life show me her body with tears in her eyes and anger in every word, as though she doesn't deserve to be cherished by someone because of something beyond her control. Let me be clear, Sky. That is false. You are beautiful, and any man would be lucky to spend his days with you."

When he broke eye contact, she sucked in a deep breath, still fighting back tears when he lowered his head to her left leg and kissed his way from her ankle to her thigh. He tenderly massaged her skin as he made his way north. She couldn't feel it as anything other than pressure, but watching him do it made those tears fall over her lashes. Land tenderly loved her other leg the same way before he positioned them again on the pillow. When he finished, he knelt on the floor and massaged her hip bones that jutted out on each side, the catheter dead center and still taped to her skin instead of coiled in her bag. His thumbs worked their way across her abdomen, stroking the skin on each side of the stoma. It was healed now to nothing more than a small hole the tube went through, and he leaned down, pressing a kiss to the skin just above it.

"Land, don't," she whispered, the tears falling at the idea of his tender touch that she couldn't feel.

"Why are you crying?" he asked, reaching up to wipe away a tear.

"I never wanted you to see me this way."

"Sweetheart, I can't tell you how much I wish you'd have talked to me. We could have worked through it together, because you are turning me on in a way I can't hide." She raised a surprised brow, and he shrugged, standing so she could see the outline of his maleness through his jeans. "My body doesn't lie, Sky."

He lowered his head again and kissed across her ribs, where there was still minimal sensation. "I can't feel you against my skin, and it's killing me," she whimpered.

In a heartbeat, he'd removed her T-shirt, pausing long enough to gaze at the lacy bra that hooked in the front. Land's growl was low and throaty when he unsnapped it and pulled it away. With all the patience and tenderness in the world, he kissed his way up to her left nipple before slipping it between his lips to tease with his tongue.

"Land!" she cried softly, arching her chest to get closer to him.

"You can feel that?" he asked, barely releasing her breast long enough to ask.

"It feels so good." She cried out again when he grasped her other nipple between his fingers and rolled it gently while he lavished her other one with his tongue. To throw her off, he switched sides, and she couldn't stop the eruption of sensation that filled her. "Land," she whimpered as the waves flowed over her. "Don't stop, please," she begged, riding the sensations high up into the sky, where she lost track of her thoughts and anything but how good it felt to be loved by this man.

When she came back to earth, he was holding her in his arms, teasing her earlobe with his tongue and teeth. "That was unexpected," he whispered, kissing her behind the ear. "Are you okay?"

"Better than okay." Her laughter was soft when she answered. "I'm literally on cloud nine. Since I don't have a lot of sensation in my lower half..." She paused, unsure what she should tell him.

"Be honest with me, angel. I want to know everything," he whispered in her ear. The sensation sent a shiver down her shoulders and pooled at her nipples again, making them tingle.

"My erogenous zones are different than other women," she explained. "I can only orgasm through intercourse if I have direct G-spot stimulation. My breasts, on the other hand, are highly orgasmic."

His soft laughter in her ear made her smile, her tears long gone after his tender loving. "I noticed. I loved every second of it, too."

"You did?" She tried to position herself so she could see him. He propped a pillow behind her back and held her waist to steady her.

Rather than answer, he held her hand to the front of his jeans. "I did." When she rubbed her hand across his hardness, his eyes rolled back in his head, and he moaned. "Is this a dream, or are you touching me right now?"

"It's not a dream unless I'm in the same one," she whispered, sliding her hand under the waistband of his pants to feel his heat. His gasp was loud when he pressed himself against her hand, his eyes closed and his body vibrating with her touch. "We can't do this."

"Do what?" she asked, grasping him through his boxers and reveling in the way his breath hitched. This was the most unexpected moment of her life, and she wanted to memorize it for when they parted ways again.

"Make love," he whispered, thrusting against her hand. "We're not prepared."

"I'm on the pill, Land."

"Not that," he whispered, grasping her hand to still her. "I refuse to endanger you for my satisfaction. After some research, I know that for a woman with a spinal cord injury to enjoy making love, planning is required or—"

"I'll have another episode of autonomic dys-reflexia?" His nod was enough for her to know he had done his research. "It's possible, but there are ways to prevent it and have a satisfying sex life."

When he took her lips, his kiss was hungry and demanding. When he finally broke for air, they were both panting. "I'm satisfied just being able to kiss and touch you, sweetheart. I don't need more right now. We can wait."

"Your body tells a different story," she whispered, squeezing his hard maleness. His moan told her she wasn't wrong.

"I just want to kiss you and hold you in my arms. It makes me feel like all the years that passed don't exist anymore."

"We can do that," she promised, unsnapping the button on his jeans without dropping his gaze. It was now or never if she wanted to show him that while a life with her might not be typical, that didn't mean it couldn't be enjoyable.

Check yourself, Skylar. There's no life with him. There's only tonight, because when the sun comes up tomorrow and reality comes float-ing back through those windows, nothing will have changed.

With all her might, she tried to ignore that voice of reason as she unzipped his pants, the chattering of the teeth sending a visible shiver through him. Just for tonight, she wanted to pretend she could have a life with this man.

"You're killing me, baby girl," he ground out, lifting his hips to lower his jeans and then his boxers.

She was holding him in a breath, his warm skin connected to hers in an elemental way that told her nothing would ever be the same be-tween them again, and she didn't want it to be. She wanted him, and all of her reasoning about why she shouldn't went out the window the mo-ment he throbbed against her. She stroked him, his hips thrusting as she did, and his moans long and low. She had no question that he was enjoying their time together. Then he cried out in pleasure, his desire throbbing rhythmi-cally in her hand as she carried him up onto his own wave of pleasure. After his release, when he gazed down at her, she saw everything he couldn't say. She prayed her eyes told him the same story.

Chapter Twenty

Reece woke slowly, his gaze taking in the woman in his arms. Sky was still naked, as was he, and they were wrapped together in a blanket he'd pulled over them after she'd made him a very happy man. She was gorgeous, all of her, and it killed him to think she believed she wasn't. If she gave him the chance, he'd tell her she was beautiful every day for the rest of his life. He suspected that would be harder to do than to say. When this was over and she had her life back, he expected her to push him away again. This time, he wouldn't let that happen.

He noticed she was still clutching her charcoal pencil and the pad lay off to the side, having fallen from her lap in sleep. She must have woken up with an idea she didn't want to forget and sketched it out. He gingerly lifted the sketch pad and paused as he went to close the book. It wasn't a mosaic she'd been sketching. It was him. His jaw dropped slightly at the image in his hands. He was alive and vibrant, even in black and white. She'd managed to represent his two different-colored eyes using only shadows and light. Stroke by stroke, she'd built him as she saw him, half the boy she used to know and half the man he had become, and married them perfectly into what he embodied as a man today. She had incredible talent, but she also had incredible insight into people and drew them from the inside out.

"Secure Watch, Whiskey." Mina's voice filled the room from his walkie-talkie, and he grabbed it carefully to avoid waking Sky. A check of the clock told him it was 2:00 a.m., which meant they'd been sleeping much longer than he'd realized.

"Secure Watch, Riker," he responded quietly.

"This is an all-call alert," Mina said. "I need you and Skylar here immediately."

"What's up?" he asked, eyeing the woman in his arms as she began to stir.

"We've got a new video. Things have escalated. Can you meet me in the conference room in ten?"

"We'll need twenty. We were sleeping, so Sky needs time to get ready."

"Ten-four."

He sat up and shifted a sleepy Sky to the pillows. "Mina doesn't do an all-call at this time of the night unless there's a massive change in the situation. We need to move."

Skylar grabbed his arm before he could leave the bed. "We need to talk, Land."

"When this is over," he said, praying the words didn't sound as harsh to her ears as they did to his. "Until you're free of this threat, that's where our concentration needs to be."

Without another word, she shifted her wheelchair and transferred into it. Watching her struggle to get her legs onto the footplate, he walked around the bed and tenderly lifted them down. She wouldn't meet his gaze, and he knew she'd heard the sharpness of his tone.

He leaned in on her wheels and forced eye contact. "Let me be clear—if I had a choice, I'd still be in that bed holding your warm body and kissing your sweet lips. First, it's my job to keep you safe and eliminate this threat. Don't misconstrue my shift in attitude to anything other than wanting to protect you and give you your life back. Got it?"

"I want the same thing, both your warm body and being free of this threat. I'll do whatever you tell me to do to make that happen."

"Good," he whispered, leaning in and stealing a kiss from her lips. "Because when this is over, we aren't going back to the lives we used to live. That's over. Fair warning."

Rather than answer, she gave him one nod and turned her chair, wheeling into the bathroom in a way that said she wasn't as convinced of that as he was. That was okay. He was a patient man. He'd waited fourteen years to be with her. He could wait a few more days.

WHEN HE AND Sky arrived at the conference room, the team was assembled, meaning this video undoubtedly changed the game.

"Sorry to rouse you so early," Mina said as a greeting, "but we've got a situation."

"How bad is it?" Reece asked, pulling a chair away from the table so Sky could roll in.

"Explosively bad," Iris said without looking away from the table. "I was on duty when it came in on the Facebook page. Whoever it is, they know we can see the page."

"Can we see the video?" Sky asked, glancing at Mina and Cal.

"I've got it ready to show you," Mina said. "Fair warning. It's traumatic, and we will protect you no matter what."

Taking her hand, Reece held it tightly between his and then nodded at Mina for her to play the video. The screen across the room lit up with a building filmed in low light. It was grainy, but they could make out a woman sitting in a wheelchair, strapped down with ropes, her mouth taped and wearing a vest. Skylar gasped.

"That's Camille Castillo!" she exclaimed.

Mina paused the video. "You're positive?"

Skylar nodded robotically. "No question. Why is she dressed like that?"

"The vest is full of explosives that can blow her and that building to kingdom come," Iris said before she grimaced. "Sorry. This is why I shouldn't talk to people."

"You're fine," Skylar said, though Reece could tell she was in shock. "I'm grateful that you tell it like it is. I can deal with that better than being lied to."

It was difficult, but Reece bit back the smile that threatened, because Sky was something else and he was glad to be the one to help her win this battle. Mina hit play again, and a familiar voice filled the room.

"Hello, Skylar. It's time we end this little tête-à-tête, don't you think? I'm sure you recognize our friend. I've been saving her for the finale." The video panned to the roof of a building with decorative brickwork.

"No," she cried. "That's the art gallery Taken for Granted. It's owned by a conglomerate of artists. We have to do something!" Skylar turned to Reece and grabbed the front of his shirt. "We have to stop him!"

While Reece tenderly grasped her hand on his shirt, Mina flicked the video back on so they could hear the rest of the message.

"I know how tight you are with this building. Last I heard, you were throwing some of that settlement money into it." The man in the mask shook his head as though he was disappointed, clucking his tongue. "Imagine how the other artists will feel if you're the reason the building comes tumbling down."

Mina paused the video again. "Is that true?"

"No," she whispered, her gaze glued to the screen. "I was asked to do a gallery showing there in a few months. I could become a partner if my work was accepted and the showing was strong. I wouldn't be using the settlement money, though. I'd use the money I saved for this reason—money that's now gone, I'm sure."

"But wait," Reece said, turning to Sky. "How many people in your life know about the settlement money?"

She tossed her head from side to side. "I suppose it wouldn't be hard to find the information online if you google the accident, but I haven't talked to anyone about the settlement money. Even when we first got the payout, we didn't discuss it. It wasn't something to celebrate or to brag about. I'd rather we hadn't needed it."

"So only people close to you know about the settlement?" Cal asked to clarify.

"Well, yeah, that or people who followed the case or were part of the accident themselves." She glanced at Reece. "Could this be one of the other accident victims?"

"Did everyone get a payout from the accident?" Cal asked, glancing at Mina with a grimace. Obviously, he had started to put things together, too.

"To a degree," Reece answered for her. "The amount depended on how serious the injury was and if the victim would have lifelong needs because of it."

"I am not a victim," Sky said between clenched teeth.

Reece pressed a kiss to her temple, not even caring what his boss thought about it. He noticed her smiling when he spoke again, though. "Not what I meant, Sky. Let me rephrase. Anyone who was injured got a payout, but it depended on their injuries. I had a broken wrist, so my bills were paid and that was it. It was the same for others who broke their arm or leg. For those who suffered traumatic brain injuries, they got a settlement that reflected the lifelong care they would need."

"That must be nice," Iris muttered with an eye roll.

"Skylar, was anyone else injured as severely as you were?" Cal asked.

"No, most suffered broken bones or cuts and bruises. Because I was in the air when the team went down, my injuries reflected the height from which I fell."

Everyone in the room grimaced at the thought as Reece took her hand again. "She's correct that anyone from that time who followed the case or was part of it would know that she got a large settlement."

"That still narrows it down considerably," Cal said. "That's a path we can follow if need be."

"Let's finish the video. Then we can hash out a plan," Mina said, clicking the remote.

The creepy voice filled the room again. "It's not too late to save Camille and your beloved building. I'll trade them for you. That seems even. Be outside the loading doors of the gallery this morning at six, alone. No cops and no security guys. If I see anyone besides you, I will blow this building and all of you sky-high. See what I did there?" His creepy horror laugh sent a shiver down Reece's spine. "There'll be a phone waiting for you there on which you'll receive a call with further instructions. If you're not there at exactly six o'clock, well, boom!

Ta-ta for now, Skylar. Tick tock, run, run...oh wait, wheel, wheel as fast as you can..."

The room went silent for a beat before everyone inhaled. "That's not happening," Reece said before anyone could speak.

"But it is," Skylar responded, turning to him. "A woman's life is on the line!"

"A woman who could be in on this!" he exclaimed in return. They stared at each other in a stalemate until Cal spoke.

"Unfortunately, we have no evidence whether Camille is or isn't in on it."

"Rather than call the police and ask for assistance," Mina said, "we tapped into the security systems around the building. We can see the side of the building where that would have been recorded, but there's no one there now."

"Am I the only one who thinks it's weird that he strapped a woman to a wheelchair, set her in front of a video camera and did a full video without anyone noticing?" Iris asked, making Reece turn toward her.

"You're right. I hadn't thought of that. It would be almost impossible to film something like that where the gallery is located in Duluth. He'd have to be quick, and I can't see that happening with a woman tied to a wheelchair like that."

"But I know that was Taken for Granted. I

have no doubt," Skylar said, shock still filling her words. "And that was Camille."

"Could the video be altered?" Reece asked Mina, who nodded with a shrug.

"That's possible. The quality is low, which could be on purpose, and the shots of her were tight to the brick. He could have spliced them together to make them look like they were at Taken for Granted," Mina said.

"We could call the bomb squad to go in, but I'm afraid he's watching the building," Cal explained. "If he sees movement and the bomb is inside the building, a lot of people would get hurt."

"We can't risk it," Skylar said, shaking her head. "Whoever this is has an issue with me and no one else. I don't want anyone to get hurt because of me. We follow his directions and don't deviate. Camille, while not my favorite person, doesn't deserve to die, and neither does anyone else. If that building blows, many other businesses and people will get hurt."

"I ran the casualty report if the building goes," Iris said, grabbing a piece of paper. "Because the gallery is located so close to the residential section of the city and the hospital, we're talking easily a billion dollars in property damage and countless lives lost if the building explodes. It's old brick, and it will fly like stone bullets."

Reece swore, his chest tight as he imagined the implications of that. "She can't be out there alone, Cal. She has no way to defend herself."

"Agreed," he said, but Sky snorted.

"He said no cops and no security guys. If he blows that building when I'm sitting in front of it, I'm dead, too."

"That's why you've got us," Roman said as he walked through the door dressed in a Secure One uniform, followed by four guys dressed the same. It was the core team of Secure One operatives.

"Skylar, my name is Efren Brenna. I believe you met my wife, Selina. This is Mack, Eric and Lucas. With all due respect, we've infiltrated a mafia kingpin's home without his knowledge. We can stake out and protect the building in question in our sleep. We got you."

Reece nodded his agreement when she glanced at him. "The team will not let you down. You can put the same amount of trust in them that you've put in me. We won't let you or anyone else get hurt, but you have to follow directions and not go rogue."

The room erupted in snickers as they glanced at Mina, who was laughing harder than any of them. "What did I miss?" Skylar asked.

Reece waved a hand in the air. "I'll tell you on the way. It's a long story. For now, will you agree to listen to the plan I know Cal has already developed and is ready to implement?"

"I'll listen, but I think I should get a say in this, too. I don't want anyone else to get hurt because of me. If anyone is going to die, it will be me."

His pulse pounding in his ears, he tipped her chin around to face him. "And you don't think that going out there and getting yourself killed would hurt me? Don't you think that watching you nearly die once was enough? Now I have to do it again?" Reece felt a nose budge against his thigh, breaking his concentration on the woman before him. He glanced down at Haven, Lucas's PTSD dog, who wasn't afraid to come to the aid of others in the group who needed a reminder not to fall too deep down a hole that would only torture them. Instinctively, he stroked Haven's head while inhaling a deep breath. "I'm sorry, but I can't do it again. We can't be reckless with your life."

"And we won't be," Cal said, trying to gain control of the situation. "Both of you need to hear me out. We can adjust the plan once you've heard it, but until then, I want your lips zipped and your eyes on me. There are a lot of moving parts and we don't have much time with a

6:00 a.m. deadline in front of us. Emotions are charged between you right now. We all feel that, but if you both trust us," he said, emphasizing *both* while holding Reece's glare, "everyone will come out of this alive."

"You have the floor," Reece said to Cal's nod. When Cal turned his back to walk to the whiteboard, Skylar slipped her hand into his and squeezed.

It was the lifeline Reece needed to focus on the plan and get her out of this safely, even if that meant he had to give her up in the end.

Chapter Twenty-One

The sky was starting to lighten ever so much as 6:00 a.m. approached. Storms were rolling in, though, and by the looks of it, they'd made it to the Duluth airport in Cal's helicopter during the calm before the storm. The Secure One team was getting into position at the art gallery and she was sitting on the sidewalk near the hospital, which was well-lit and patrolled by security. The gallery was across the street and down a few blocks but close enough that she could wheel herself to it.

The team wanted her to arrive at the gallery at 5:58 a.m., giving them time to get into place and prevent this criminal from coming in hot before they were prepared. He was surely watching the building, but she had confidence the guys could still infiltrate it without him knowing. Who this was, she still didn't know. With Miles and Silas dead and Camille tied up in the chair, it had to be someone from her past that she wasn't aware had a grudge against her. The idea that someone would do all of this because of money was hard to swallow, even more so if it was someone from their cheer team. Reece had assured her that it wasn't her fault. This rested directly on the shoulders of the person behind the mask, and when he was caught—and they would catch him—he'd answer for his crimes to the fullest extent of the law.

Before they left, Iris had told them that the Facebook page, including all the videos and the petition page, had disappeared. That proved the person behind this knew what they were doing in the digital world and didn't want to leave a trail for the authorities to follow. Unfortunately for them, Secure Watch had multiple backups of all the videos and the petition page. Once this guy was unmasked, he wouldn't wiggle out of this one.

Nervous, Skylar shifted in her chair and checked her watch. It was time to get rolling if she would make her deadline. All she could see was the pain in Land's eyes when he lowered her to her chair when they arrived at the hospital parking ramp. His blue eye was filled with so much hope, while his gray eye was filled with pain, fear and worry. Her demand to do this had cut him deeply and made him bleed again, something she hated but couldn't prevent. Having him back in her life had been fantastic despite the circumstances, but he couldn't remain there. She never wanted to be the reason he hurt again.

You don't think shutting him out of your life again won't cut him deeply?

That voice was back at a time when she needed to hear it the least. To avoid focusing on that thought, she snapped her brakes off and pushed forward, the slight incline distracting her from thinking about anything other than making it to the gallery in time to answer the call from a lunatic she couldn't see and didn't know.

Headlights illuminated the street and nearly blinded her as they came around the corner toward the hospital at a high rate of speed. Someone must be in trouble. Sky turned her head to block the light as she pushed her rims, but she was suddenly snapped backward and flailing in the air. She landed hard on her side as a door slid shut. An engine gunned, and she rolled to the side until her head slammed up against metal to stop her.

"Well, well, who do we have here?" a voice asked. For the first time since all of this began, she recognized it, and her insides gelled.

"RIKER IN PLACE," Reece said into his walkie.

"Ten-four," Cal answered. "We're in position. Everything is quiet here. We have confirmation on the phone waiting by the loading dock."

"What are the chances that when it rings, the place blows?"

"From what we can tell, there are no explosives inside the building. If there are, they're well hidden."

"It's more likely a bullet will be headed her way once she's in position," Reece ground out, his heart pounding. "I don't like this, Charlie. There are too many variables."

"None of us disagree," he responded. "You need to trust us as much as she trusts you, okay? Love and fear are equally powerful emotions, but you can't let either one take control of the situation."

"Don't believe love was ever mentioned in any context here, Charlie," Reece responded as he watched Sky from his position.

He heard Cal snort softly when he released the button on his walkie. "If you think it needed to be mentioned, then you're more delusional than I thought. You two make more googly eyes at each other than Roman and Mina, and we all thought they were bad. You two are insufferable."

"Charlie?" Reece asked, releasing the button.

"Yeah, Riker?"

"Shut up," he said, then released the button to hear several snickers.

"Secure Watch, Whiskey," Mina broke in. "I

hate to break this up, but we have a situation." Mina had stayed at command central to run their coms and keep them abreast of any communication that may come in from this guy. "Charlie, your PD contact just called. They just got the DNA match back on the body thought to be Miles Bradshaw. It's not him."

"What?" Reece asked, leaning forward in the van seat. "I thought he'd already been identified."

"Only using the identification on the body. The face and hands suffered so much trauma they had to run DNA to be sure. The person they found is a known felon from the area who had been living on the streets."

"Dammit!" Reece growled as he noticed Sky snap the brakes off her chair. "The package is on the move. We've got to stop her. This is a trap! Miles has to be the one behind the mask."

"If we stop her, we can't predict what he will do," Cal said, and Reece heard the hesitation in his voice.

"She's cresting the hill," he said. "We don't have much time to decide." He'd barely finished the sentence when a van came around the corner going way too fast. It clipped the curb as it came to a stop, and before his eyes, the occupant pulled Sky from her wheelchair and dumped her into the van before rocketing down the hill.

"Oh, hell no!" he yelled, jamming the SUV into gear and screaming into the walkie-talkie a description of the van. "I'm in pursuit, but I need backup! They're headed to I-35!"

"Stay on them!" Cal yelled as Reece dropped the walkie to put both hands on the wheel. The van ran a yellow at the first set of lights, and he didn't brake. He ran the red, the screech of brakes filling his ears but not breaking his concentration. The next set of lights turned green just as the van reached it and roared through. Reece nearly caught up as they turned past Leif Erikson Park, but the van's brake lights lit up. Then it sailed to the right toward the park, barely missing the giant statute of Leif before it went airborne and soared into the park until it rolled twice and came to rest on the roof near the shore of Lake Superior.

Reece ran toward the van, screaming Sky's name as he drew his gun. The wheels of the van spun in the air as he aimed his gun at the passenger window, expecting to see crumpled bodies where there were none.

"Sky!" When he finally spotted her, she was crumpled against the side of the van on the driver's side. He pulled the sliding door open, the creak and groan of bent metal sending a shiver down his spine.

He caught motion from the side of his eye as someone barreled toward him. Reece raised his arm to block the guy, but he took a punch to his head, knocking him back a step. They tussled, but the other man was no match for Reece, who quickly subdued him after a bit of grappling. He had his knee in his back when Cal ran up with Mack and Eric. Cal slapped a pair of cuffs on the guy before he stood him up then Mack ripped his mask off.

Reece registered the face of Miles Bradshaw before he practically ripped the door off the van and crawled toward the woman he'd loved his entire life, now crumpled in a heap on the roof of the van. "Sky. Angel," he said, gently slapping her face. "Wake up, please. Don't do this to me again. You have to wake up. I love you. Wake up so I can see those beautiful blue eyes of yours fill with anger when I tell you that I love you and I'm never letting you out of my sight ever again. I don't care if that makes you mad. We were meant for each other, and it's time to stop pretending that's not true. Skylar, please." He checked her pulse as he pleaded with her, pleased when it was strong and steady.

"Reece, I need you to move so I can assess

her," Selina said, crowding into the space next to him.

"No, I'm not leaving her."

"I didn't ask you to. I need you to move toward her head and hold it carefully to protect her neck while I check her vital signs."

Doing what she asked was easier said than done, but he finally managed to shift himself into the space between Sky's head and the back of the driver's seat. "Come on, angel. Wake up." He heard an ambulance in the distance, and a little of the tension in his belly was released. As if on command, her eyes fluttered open, and she gazed into his with a blank stare for several seconds.

After she blinked twice, she gasped. "Land."

"It's okay, Skylar," Selina said, holding her shoulder so she didn't try to move. "The ambulance is on its way, and they'll take you to the hospital to assess you. Does your neck hurt?"

"No," Skylar said, staring at him with big, round blue eyes. "My neck is fine. I swear the guy who pulled me into the van sounded just like Miles, but he's dead!"

"He's not," Reece said quickly. "His identification was planted on the body, but it wasn't him. We got him. He's cuffed and waiting for the cops."

Sky moaned when Selina pressed on her side.

"Something hurts, but I can't tell you what." Selina lifted her hands off her body. "There were two guys. Miles was the one who tossed me inside, but there was a driver. The driver never spoke."

"I'm going to get the EMTs," Selina said, ducking out of the van and leaving Reece to hold Sky steady.

"How did the van crash?" he asked, holding her gaze. He couldn't help but notice her eyes were displaying signs of a concussion.

"I couldn't let them take me, Land. I was afraid if they got too far away, you'd never find me alive. Miles left me on the floor, thinking I couldn't move, and got in the front seat. I pulled myself forward with my arms and grabbed the wheel. We weren't going fast yet, so I thought it would be safe. I didn't realize we'd roll the way we did. I'm sorry. I'm sorry I didn't listen when you told me not to trust them. I should have trusted you."

"Shh," he soothed, kissing her forehead. "You're okay. We've got Miles. As soon as you're in the ambulance, I'll tell Cal about the driver and then meet you at the hospital. Okay? Just stay calm."

Shouting ensued as the EMTs arrived to transport her a few blocks to the hospital. Reece moved aside to give them room to work and pulled Cal aside.

"How's Skylar?"

"She's hurting, but she doesn't know where. It's probably her ribs, but she doesn't have full innervation, so that's making it easier for her to tolerate the pain. She was able to wrestle the wheel from them and crash the van, but the driver somehow got away before I got there."

"That girl has moxie," Cal said with a grin. "Do you think it was Camille?"

"She's the only player left in the game," he agreed. "I have to go to the hospital with her. She's a sitting duck if Camille shows up."

"Go. Don't let Skylar out of your sight. I'll update you about Camille once Miles squeals on his partner."

"If he squeals on her."

"He will," Cal assured him with a wink.

Motioning behind him, Reece sighed. "I hate to leave you with this mess to sort out."

"Go," he said, pointing to the ambulance with his robotic finger. You didn't argue with Cal when he gave a direct order with that finger. "This is child's play compared to the messes I've cleaned up over the last few years. I'll send some guys to the hospital once I can spare them. Keep me updated on your location."

"You got it, boss." He saluted and took off for

the van, where they were pulling out the woman he loved on a backboard. He wanted to crumple at the memory of the same scene repeating itself from fourteen years ago, and he tripped, putting his arms out to break his fall when a strong hand grabbed him instead.

"Head in the game, Riker," Cal whispered. "She needs you to keep her calm and be her advocate right now. It'll be hard, but you can fall apart later. Push everything else aside and concentrate on the second chance you've been given."

He took a deep breath in and exhaled on four. "Thanks, Charlie."

Cal slapped him on the back and returned to the team while he headed toward his second chance.

Chapter Twenty-Two

The machines beeped in alternating rhythms and reminded Skylar of all the days and nights she'd spent in the hospital over the years. Today, though, they reminded her that she was a survivor and had saved herself.

She'd been paralyzed with fear when he threw her against the side of the van, but terror had ripped through her when she recognized Miles's voice. He was supposed to be dead, but there he was, taking her only God knew where, and she was the only person who could stop it. She'd used the momentum to slide forward on the cargo van floor toward the driver's seat as they flew down the hill. She'd had one chance to push herself up and grab the wheel. It was a risk and she could have died, but she'd hadn't known Reece was right behind her then, so she'd had no choice. Even lying in a hospital bed with broken ribs and a fractured pelvis, she didn't regret it. She was alive because she took a chance.

If only she could find the same courage to take a chance with Land. Until a few moments ago, he hadn't left her side since they'd pulled her from the van nearly six hours ago. He'd kept in contact with Cal and the team as they tried to find the driver, but so far, nothing. It didn't help that Miles wasn't talking about the identity of his companion. Even when the cops read the list of charges against him, including first-degree murder, he'd refused to answer any of their questions. That was his right, but it wouldn't end well for him. Then again, as far as she was concerned, that was fitting for a man like Miles Bradshaw.

Now that Land had stepped out of the room to take a call from Mina, she thought back to the first few moments in the van when she'd started to come around after the crash. He'd been begging her to wake up by telling her he loved her. He hadn't said it since she opened her eyes, and she wondered if it had just been a ploy to get her to wake up. The thing was, it had sounded sincere to her concussed ears. He'd also looked sincere when she opened her eyes and gazed into his, filled with worry and fear. That emotion she could never name before was also there, and that was the moment she'd realized she could name it. Love. It was love. Somehow, she had to find the courage to open up her soul and say the words back. Let him know she'd heard him and felt the same way.

Skylar had accepted one thing on the short ambulance ride to the hospital with Land holding her hand the whole way. She wanted a chance with him—deserved a chance with him—and nothing else mattered.

There was a knock on the door. "Phlebotomy," a voice said, and she called for them to come in. A man dressed in scrubs stepped inside the room wearing a surgical mask and carrying a tool kit.

"Are you sure you have the right room?" she asked when he set the tub on the bedside table. "Someone just drew my blood about thirty minutes ago."

"I'm positive I've got the right room," he said as he lowered his mask. The man before her had a giant bruise covering the left side of his face, but she didn't need to see that side to recognize him.

"Silas?"

"You act surprised, little sister." He frowned in an exaggerated, scary dipping of his lips. "Let me guess, our mutual friend found the article about my untimely death? I figured if anyone was going to uncover that little tidbit, it would be him. He always stuck his nose where it didn't belong."

This wasn't good. If her brother was in the room, that meant Land hadn't seen him come in or Silas had done something to him.

"Did you hurt Reece?"

Her brother made the same sarcastic snorting sound he'd made since they were kids. "No, I didn't touch a hair on his pretty little head. He was talking on the phone, completely ignoring your room. I'm sure he's tired of all your dramatics by now. God knows I am."

It looked like she would have to be her own hero again, but this time, it would be much harder to beat the man before her. She'd have to keep him talking until she figured out a plan.

"THANKS FOR ARRANGING their flights, Mina," Reece said from the lounge. He had a full view of Sky's door and was watching it, but he didn't want her to overhear him talking to Mina. "I know Sky's mom won't sleep until she has seen her with her own two eyes. We also want to tell them about Silas in person."

"Do you think they'll be surprised to learn he's dead?"

"Logically? No. Emotionally? Yes. They're his parents, regardless of everything that's happened. I think it's fair to say it will still be a gut punch."

"True," Mina agreed. "Lucas stayed behind

with Haven. He's on his way to the hospital now to help you keep an eye on Sky's room. When it's time for their flight to arrive, he'll meet them at the airport and bring them to the hospital. We thought Haven might be a useful addition to the party."

Reece sighed and rubbed a hand over his face. "Tell Cal I'm fine."

"Haven is a calming presence when emotions are high and people are facing memories of the past, so we thought he'd be useful when they learned their son was dead. That said, the fact you felt the need to tell me you're fine concerns me."

He shook his head with a smile. "I had a moment after the accident, but Cal was there and set me back on the right path. I'm good now."

"Cal's good at that," she agreed.

"Tell Lucas we're on floor five West. If he texts me when he's in the parking garage, I'll run down and meet him."

"You won't do that. I don't want you to leave her there alone. I've already sent him her room number. He'll meet you there."

"Whatever you say, boss," he said with a smirk.

"Tell Sky we're all looking forward to the day when we can share dinner with her again. Sadie is itching to cook for her to help her heal."

"I'll tell her. Thanks for everything, Mina. You've all gone above and beyond for someone you had never met."

"We didn't need to meet her, Reece. She was yours, which made her ours. That's what makes us Secure One."

"I still feel fortunate to be part of this team." He noticed an orderly with a toolbox in his hand knock on Sky's door before he entered. "It looks like they're back for more blood on Sky. I better go check on her."

"Tell her we're rooting for her. Whiskey, out," she said, and the line went dead before he could respond.

Reece stood and stretched, his back sore from the hours of sitting once the adrenaline had drained away. The CT scans on Sky had shown broken ribs and a fractured pelvis, not to mention the concussion, but she was going to be okay. They'd keep her in the hospital for at least a week to treat the fractures and prevent bed sores from developing. Once she was released to home, she'd need specially made cushions in her chair and bed that would prevent sores while she finished healing. Despite her osteoporosis, the doctors were confident the fractures would heal well if she took the new medication to promote bone healing and followed their orders. Knowing her injuries wouldn't give her any problems in the future was a relief to hear after the day they'd had.

The one elephant in the room that hadn't been addressed was his declaration of love inside the van. He couldn't be sure she'd heard him, so rather than say anything while she had a head injury and was in pain, he decided to wait until tomorrow—unless she said something today. Cowardly? Yes, but he wasn't ready to deal with Sky trying to push him away again. She would try, but he wouldn't allow it. He just needed a day to be with her without making her angry.

He stood to the side of the door and listened, not wanting to walk in and distract the person with a needle in her arm. They had just drawn blood a bit ago, so it was strange they were back, but in a hospital, you came to expect the unexpected.

"Why, Silas? Why do all this?" he heard Sky ask, and his blood ran cold. Silas? He was dead. Was she dreaming? Was the head injury worse than initially thought?

Ready to run in, he paused when a man spoke and he recognized the voice. "The answer is simple. Revenge. From the day you were born, I spent my childhood in your shadow, and I was the oldest," the man shouted, lowering his voice before he spoke again. "It was really annoying when that accident didn't kill you. I did take great pleasure in knowing you'd never have a normal life and, at the same time, I destroyed the life of Reece Palmer. Honestly, that was the only balm when you survived."

"Wait, you caused the accident that night on the field? How? You weren't driving the golf cart."

Reece pulled out his phone and sent a text with three letters: SOS. Then, he opened his recording app and hit Record before he pulled his gun from his holster.

"See, this is so typical. Everyone thinks I was too stupid to know basic things like how to cut the brake lines on a golf cart. That was child's play, little sis. Then you drug the person driving it and wait for the carnage to ensue."

"You're a monster," she said. Reece heard the sound of skin slapping, and then Sky gasped.

"I am a monster, and now is my chance to finish what I started fourteen years ago. Thank God, as I'm tired of this game."

"Who did you hire to obliterate me from the internet?" Sky asked.

"Again, I'm not as dumb as you all thought I was. You've heard about online classes now, right? They're easy to sign up for with a fake identification, and since you never have to show up to class, no one really knows who's behind that computer. In a matter of a year, I'd graduated with a degree in cybersecurity, just like your little lover boy." He said the words with so much venom it sent a shiver through Reece.

"Were you the one behind the mask in the videos?"

"Iconic, right?" Silas asked as though he should get an Oscar for his performances. "It was such fun. I wanted to make more but, alas, it's time to end this now."

Silas was right about one thing. It was time to end this. "Stop right there, Silas," he said, swinging into the room with his gun pointed at the man holding a hypodermic needle.

Silas spun in surprise but didn't drop the needle in his hand. "Cripes. Not you again. I should have killed you before I put all this into motion. I never dreamed my baby sister would call you after shunning you for fourteen years, but what they say must be true. Our past always comes back to haunt us."

"Put the needle down and back away from the bed, Silas," he said, walking toward the man who'd grabbed Sky's intravenous line and held the needle near the port.

"I don't think you're in any position to give orders, Reece. Now, put the gun down on the floor and back up. This is between me and my sister. You've got no place here."

He had to think fast if he was going to keep

him from injecting whatever was in that syringe into her vein.

"I mean it," Silas growled. "There's enough fentanyl in this needle to kill her three times. Put the gun down."

That was not the answer he wanted. Reece glanced at Sky, who nodded for him to do it, but he caught the way she flicked her gaze down and followed it, noting she had the call button in her hand, her thumb hovering over it. Whatever she was planning, between his SOS and her, maybe they'd get out of this alive. They just had to keep him talking.

"Okay," Reece said, lowering the gun to the floor and kicking it to the edge of her bed, his hands in the air. "You don't want to hurt anyone else here. Where's Camille?"

Silas rolled his eyes but lowered the syringe a hair with the motion. "Wasn't it Gordon Lightfoot who said the Lady of the Lake never gives up her dead?" His laughter was deranged before he spoke again. "She went overboard somewhere between Two Harbors and Grand Marais. The wheelchair and vest full of rocks probably didn't help her float."

"Were you going to kill Miles after he helped you get Sky?"

"Miles." He spat the name like it was poison. "Such a whiny crybaby." He motioned around in the air with the needle. "He was one of those guys who wanted all the credit for doing very little. I'm over here working hard to take care of my problems and he wants to cry about how my sister is better than him. It was sickening. I wish I'd had time to end him earlier, but of course, there you were to save the day again and I had to disappear. He won't last long in prison."

"Neither will you," Reece said, raising a brow. "Especially in the general population. Then again, maybe you'll end up in an institution for the criminally insane. Seeing as how you've killed four people now? At least?"

"Four?" Sky asked, glancing between them. "You mean two, right?"

"Two that we know of," Reece answered. "I'm betting that your grandparents' deaths in Nebraska weren't accidental."

"Well, look at the investigative cojones on Reece Palmer," Silas said, his words dripping with sarcasm. He scrunched up his nose for a moment. "It was almost too easy to knock those two off, but satisfying nonetheless. When I finish here, I'll have to pay Mommy and Daddy dearest a visit."

"You killed our grandparents?" Sky asked, her words dripping with shock and disdain.

"You weren't the one who had to suffer

through multiple summers listening to that old windbag go on about how repenting to Jesus was the answer to all my problems. I made sure he met Jesus, that's all." Silas shrugged as though it was completely normal.

The curtain billowed back as a nurse walked in. "I'm here with your…"

The intrusion drew Silas's attention, and Reece took his chance, charging the man, head down, until he slammed into him. They went down to the floor, Reece trying to prevent Silas from stabbing him with the needle. The nurse was at the door screaming for security, and Sky kept screaming his name repeatedly while Silas grunted.

Reece swung at him with his right fist just as Silas moved, and the needle jabbed him between two tendons in his hand. "Night-night," Silas sang right before he hit the plunger. The last thing Reece remembered was the look of terror on Sky's face when she realized what had happened.

Chapter Twenty-Three

"Where's Reece?" Skylar had asked the same question for an hour and a half, but no one would answer. "Lucas!" she exclaimed in frustration as he stood guard at the door of her room.

Haven whined and nudged her hand with his nose until she smoothed a hand over his soft head, each stroke calming her. She drew a deep breath and let it out again, reminding herself it wasn't Secure One's fault that Reece got hurt. That was her fault.

Her room had turned into pandemonium when Silas stuck that needle into Reece's hand. Security had wrestled her brother off Reece while the nurse administered Narcan to the man she loved. EMTs ran in and hauled Reece away before she got a chance to see if Narcan had reversed the effect of the drug. It had been an excruciating ninety minutes waiting to hear if Reece was okay. Added to the worry was that no one could confirm if Camille was actually dead or if she was waiting in the wings for their final swan song.

There were voices in the hallway, and then Lucas spoke. "Haven, return." The dog gave her one last nose boop and then trotted to his handler before they disappeared out the door. Selina walked in with a smile on her face, which, in some way, gave Skylar hope that Land would be all right.

"Hi," Selina said, grabbing a chair and pulling it over to sit by her. "Has anyone given you an update on Reece?"

"No," she answered, her lip trembling. "I don't even know if he's alive."

"He's doing fine," Selina assured her immediately, patting her hand. "They need to observe him a bit longer in the ER before he can be with you. They're currently testing the syringe to see what the drug mixture was that Silas gave him. Narcan reversed it, so it was certainly an opioid, but they're often mixed with other things these days, and it's important to know what. Since it was injected into his hand, they're worried about abscesses or injury to the soft tissue. His hand will be wrapped to prevent infection until they know. I wanted to warn you, but it's just a precaution until they know what drugs Silas gave him."

"My brain is struggling to wrap itself around all of this," she admitted.

"It's probably the concussion," Selina said with a wink. "Bottom line—Reece will be fine in a few hours. He's in the ER yelling about getting back up here, so my medical opinion is he's out of the woods."

Her head was definitely sore after the number of times she'd smacked it on the metal of the cargo van, but that wasn't the problem. "My brother hated me so much that he caused trauma to an entire team of teenagers to get revenge. How do I live with that?"

"Don't forget he changed your life in irreparable ways when he hatched that plan," Selina added.

Forcing back an eye roll, Skylar huffed. "Gee, thanks for the reminder."

The woman beside her bed shrugged. "I like to keep it real, and this is about as real as it gets. You have to know this wasn't your fault, though, right? Your brother had serious mental health issues that caused him to hallucinate things that weren't true and then fixate on them."

"I know what schizophrenia does to the brain, Selina. That doesn't mean I don't feel responsible for every injury and death that's occurred since that day on the field."

"You shouldn't," Selina said firmly. "First of all, he's not your son. He's a sibling who abused you and caused you unbelievable pain and suffering throughout your childhood. Your parents failed you and your brother multiple times over the years, but even they aren't responsible for his choices once he was an adult. They got him help, right?"

"Yes," Skylar agreed. "The gamut, including a stint of inpatient therapy. Nothing seemed to help for very long."

"Not unusual," Selina agreed. "But here's the thing, Skylar. Everything that happened was the result of *his* choices, not yours."

"You're saying I've suffered enough and waging psychological warfare on myself about this is unjust?"

"Yep," she agreed with a wink. "You deserve a little bit of happiness in life. I hope you've found that now and never let it go."

If Selina was talking about Land, she had to be delusional. There was no way he was going to be with her after this. Not only had her family tried to kill him twice, but now everyone in this town would know what Silas had done and how many people he maimed and hurt. She moaned, throwing her hand over her eyes in despair.

"What is it? Are you in pain?" Selina asked, standing from the chair to check her machines.

"No." Skylar moaned the word more than she spoke it. "I realized there's no way I can stay in this town. There'll be a trial, and our skeletons will be paraded around for the world to see. No one will host or buy my art here ever again."

Selina squeezed her shoulder gently. "Maybe it's time for a new name and town then. Just keep an open mind. Remember, you didn't do this and don't carry any responsibility for it. You're the victim and Silas is the perpetrator. The public will see that's true once the trial begins."

Skylar nodded, but it was more for show than agreement. She wasn't sure Selina was right, but she meant well, and for that, she was grateful. "Thanks, Selina. I'll think about that. It sounds like I've got at least a week in this place, so I'll have plenty of time on my hands."

"All of us at Secure One and Secure Watch are proud of you for being your own hero when the chips were down. Not everyone would have been that strong or quick on their feet."

"Or, in this case, quick on their belly," Skylar said, laughter escaping her lips. "I couldn't let them win."

"Because you didn't want to die?"

Skylar tipped her head side to side for a few

moments before answering. "Death is always coming for us, Selina. I didn't want to accept it before I had a chance at a life with Land. That's what drove me to grab that wheel. The chance that we could be something despite all the history between us. I might have made a different decision if I knew Silas was behind that mask and all the carnage he'd caused."

"No, you wouldn't have," Selina said, standing and squeezing her shoulder again. "Everyone deserves a chance at happiness in their life, Skylar. When Reece comes to you, please keep an open mind and remember that he doesn't blame you for what happened. You've always been his hero. Today, you reminded him of why. I'm going to check on him, and I'll send Lucas a text with how he is. You get some rest."

"Okay, thanks, Selina," Skylar whispered, waving as the woman left her room and Lucas took his place outside her door.

Skylar gazed out the window at the lake beyond and sighed. Selina was right. It was time for a new name and town, but they wouldn't include Land. He had suffered enough because of her. Despite their lifelong connection, she couldn't let him throw the rest of his life away. Resolved, she closed her eyes and let the tears fall. They weren't the first ones she'd cried for Reece Palmer, and they wouldn't be the last, but she'd take the suffering if it meant he could be happy. After all these years, he deserved that more than anyone.

IT WAS LATE when Reece returned to Sky's floor, but he paused at the end of the hallway to look down the hill and out over the lake. It was ironic that he could see the accident site from where he was, but he chose to focus on the thousand-foot laker that was headed into port. It was an iconic image of the Twin Ports and one he'd grown up with, but things were changing, and he had to be willing to change with them.

He pushed the door open to Sky's room and noticed only the small light to the side of her bed was on. It cast a glow across her that reminded him why he always called her his angel. Tonight, seeing her wearing a custom pelvic brace made at her bedside and connected to machines that beeped and hissed, he had never loved her more. From what Selina had told him, he'd have to work hard to prove that to her.

Her eyes were closed and her face was blotchy, and he expected when she opened those sweet blue eyes, they'd be bloodshot from tears. Tears she'd cried over losing him for the second time in her life. That wasn't going to happen. Not on his watch.

"Hi, angel," he whispered, kissing her temple. "I know you're awake, so open those beautiful eyes for me."

"I need to rest," she said, her voice raspy from the tears. "The doctors said I'll heal faster."

With a smile, he pulled a chair over and sat down. "Angel, look at me."

When she opened her eyes, she proved him right, and his gut clenched to know she'd been alone, in pain and crying. He should have been holding her. "Selina said you're going to be okay."

"I am," he agreed as he held up his hand. "The doctors bandaged it with some antibacterial wrap until they know what the drugs were in the needle. I feel fine, so I'm confident all will be well, but I'll wear this until the results return."

"I'm so sorry," she whispered, her chin and lips trembling as she gazed at his hand rather than make eye contact. "I'm so, so sorry."

He couldn't stand the guardrail between them, so he lowered it and slid his hand under hers to hold it loosely. "Sweetheart, stop apologizing. None of this was your fault. Silas is a disturbed individual. He's the very definition of the criminally insane. They've got him on twenty-four-hour suicide watch while they try to find someplace to send him that can handle his extensive needs."

"My parents," she whispered, tears falling from her cheeks. "They're going to be so torn apart by this."

Reece knew they'd be surprised, but more than likely, they'd be more angry than torn apart. Their son had killed his mother's parents. There would be animosity and anger, but Reece knew the love was already gone.

"Your parents are on their way here. I was returning to tell you that Mina had gotten them on a plane to Duluth when the Silas situation happened. They'll arrive in the morning and Lucas will bring them to you. I'll also be here to help answer questions."

"No, you won't be," she said, her voice breaking. "You have to go, Land. You have to go and live your life without me. You don't want any part of the trial that's about to happen, much less to associate with a Sullivan in this town."

This would be tougher than even he'd thought it would be. Once he'd raised the head of her bed, he got a washcloth and wiped her face, letting the warmth soak into her cheeks. After she'd settled again and he'd gotten her a drink of water, he sat on the edge of her bed and took her hand.

"There likely won't be a trial, Sky. It's doubtful they'd find a psychiatrist who would consider him mentally competent."

After taking a calming breath and clearing her throat, she finally held his gaze. "What will happen then? They can't let him go."

"No, Silas will never see freedom again. He'll be sent to a maximum-security hospital for the criminally insane, where he will stay until he's either fit to stand trial or dead."

"That makes me feel slightly better," she sighed. "I don't know that I'll ever get over all the hurt Silas caused, Land. What did I do to make him so angry?" she asked, poking herself in the chest.

"Nothing," he promised, wiping another tear. She'd been through so much the last week, and he just wanted to do anything to make it better for her. "Silas has been sick his entire life. There's no blame or fault to be had here. You have two choices. You can move forward and live your life doing as much good in the world as possible, or you can dwell on the past in a lonely, solitary world. I don't see any justice in the latter, do you?"

Her head shook, but her lips still trembled when she spoke. "No, I don't. The problem is that this will taint my future. No one will buy art from a Sullivan ever again. Not in this town or anywhere."

He tipped his head side to side while considering what she said. "I don't know if that's true or untrue. Some people probably wouldn't, but I would venture to guess that most people won't hesitate. That said, maybe it's time for a change in name and place."

"What, like using my mom's maiden name or something? I suppose I could do that, but finding a new living situation would be tough."

Fishing in his pocket, he pulled out a box. "I had a different name in mind." The box opened, and a diamond solitaire sparkled back at her. "I think Skylar Palmer has a nice ring to it. Always have."

"You— Is that an engagement ring?" she asked, her lips struggling to form the words.

"It is," he said, swiping another tear off her cheek with the bandage on his hand. "The diamond is a bit small, but it's what I could afford fourteen years ago when I bought it. We'll consider it a placeholder until you're well enough to go with me to pick out one you'd like."

"I'm so confused," she whispered. "How did you get a ring when you've been in the ER?"

"Friends," he said with a wink. "Once I explained to Cal how to find it, he was there and back in less time than it should take to get to my house from here."

"Sounds like Cal," she said, and this time her lips were smiling.

"Technically, I should wait until your dad is

here to ask his permission, but since he gave that to me fourteen years ago, the same answer probably still applies."

"Wait, what? You were going to ask me to marry you after high school?"

"I was," Reece said with a nod. "See, I love you, Skylar Sullivan. I have for just about forever. That's why I'm sitting here at thirty-one, still single and holding out a ring I bought when I was eighteen. It seemed to me this was always where we'd end up. Then, now, it didn't matter—this was our destiny."

"You've kept the ring all this time?" she asked in awe, her gaze drifting to the box he held up again.

"And I'm glad I did, given where I sit tonight. Skylar Ann Sullivan, will you please marry me? I've wanted nothing more than to love and hold you every day for the last fourteen years. There's no reason to wait another day."

"But, Land, I have to leave town," she whispered, leaning forward slightly from the bed until she remembered her broken ribs. "As sad as it makes me, I can't stay here after all this."

"Well, I did accept a new job today. Okay, a new old job, but it does require me to relocate."

"To a little cabin behind a big security fence?" she asked, her lips tilted upward.

"At least for the foreseeable future," he

agreed. "Imagine having a little studio in a place where inspiration is everywhere you turn."

"That's easy to imagine. So is a life with you, Land. Always has been, but I was too afraid that you'd give up opportunities in life because of my disability."

"Angel, I would give up any opportunity for you, because that's what love is. Ask yourself if you'd do the same for me."

"I don't need to ask myself that. The answer is yes. That's why I pushed you away all those years ago and planned to do it again tonight. I love you, Reece Palmer. I've loved you since the first day I met you, but it took me too long to understand that I deserved that kind of love."

"You, more than anyone I've ever known, deserve all the love in the world," he whispered, taking the ring from the box and sliding it onto her finger.

Her brow went up. "I haven't said yes."

"You did," he said, his heart pounding with joy and happiness to see that ring nestled on her finger. "You said, 'The answer is yes,' just a moment ago."

"I meant about if I'd give up the world for you."

"In my opinion, that answered my question."

Sky's smile grew as she gazed at the ring, the

lights from above making it sparkle each time she moved her hand. "I like how it looks, but the way it feels is even better."

"How does it feel?" he asked, leaning in to steal a kiss from her lips but pausing so she could answer.

"Like love," she whispered, and he waited no longer to start the first kiss of the rest of their lives.

* * * * *

Get up to 4 Free Books!

**We'll send you 2 free books from each series you try
PLUS a free Mystery Gift.**

FREE Value Over **$25**

Both the **Harlequin Intrigue®** and **Harlequin® Romantic Suspense** series
feature compelling novels filled with heart-racing action-packed romance
that will keep you on the edge of your seat.